MW01125326

# Romance Collection

A work of fiction by Terry Atkinson

Originally written as a collection of three short romances, I've expanded this collection to twelve sweet, clean and wholesome reads. Enjoy!

# Table of Contents

# Romantic Rain

Cassie stirred from her deep sleep to the sound of the rain pattering on the tin roof. She rolled over, reaching out to put her arm around the broad shoulders of Mike, the love of her life. She was half asleep and fumbled, seeking the familiar warmth of his strong body. Finding emptiness, she wriggled closer to snuggle against him while the rain pitter-pattered gently with its natural percussion on the roof.

But something didn't feel right. In her dozy state, she sensed something awry. Awakeness slowly filtered through her awareness, forcing the dreams out of her busy mind. She opened her eyes and made out some dim shapes in the dark room. It was darker than usual due to the loaded clouds and their contents obscuring any chance of the pre-dawn light glimmering through the curtains.

As her eyes got accustomed to the darkness, she saw that Mike's bulky form was not anywhere in sight. Her attempts to cuddle and snuggle in the cosy warmth had been in vain. "Mike?" she called softly, thinking he might also

have been woken by the rain and could be up and about, not able to sleep. No answer. The rain steadily beat down on the tin roof - she would have to call with more volume to be heard, or she'd need to get up if she wanted her cuddle.

As Cassie had been enjoying such a deep and peaceful sleep, full of sweet and playful dreams, she was very reluctant to leave the cosy warmth of her bed. She decided to turn over and close her eyes and enjoy the rhythm of the rain soothing her back to sleep.

But sleep just wouldn't come back to Cassie now that she'd woken and could hear the rain. She thought she'd just rest a while until Mike climbed back into bed. It was far too warm and cosy to get up and join him. She lay there listening to the drumming rain hoping Mike would join her soon. Too tired to do anything but lie there and listen to the rain, and too awake to drift back to sleep, Cassie waited... and waited...

After some time, she started to get anxious. Mike still hadn't come back to bed.

Now she really couldn't sleep and also couldn't relax. Reluctantly, she pushed back the duvet and slipped out of their comfy king-sized bed. Leaning across to the bedside table she switched on the night lamp next to the bed. Slipping on her warm slippers, she made her way out of the bedroom.

"Mike, are you downstairs?" she called from the top of the wooden stairway. Not a sound. She quickly checked Mike's office next to their main room but no sign. The bathroom was empty too. Putting on the lights for the stairway, Cassie made her way quickly down the stairs, feeling her heart beating faster with anxiety. She didn't like being alone and this was most strange, that Mike was nowhere to be found and not answering.

Suddenly, there he was - standing in the hallway just outside the kitchen, the kitchen light casting magnified shadows of his already huge frame against the wall behind. "Mike! You scared me! Didn't you hear me calling? I thought you'd disappeared into the night!"

"Hey Honey! Sorry. I don't think I'll be disappearing fast out there in all that rain! I was in the kitchen with the door closed because I had the light on and didn't want to disturb you."

"What are you getting up to, in the kitchen before dawn on this rainy night?"

Mike looked lovingly at his beloved Cassie. To the degree that Mike was a well-built, strapping chap, Cassie was slight and almost waif-like despite the fact that she could eat like a horse. They always laughed about that. Cassie didn't care. She'd rather have it that way round than have a struggle to keep the weight off. Besides, she only ate when she was hungry, and it was usually good old-fashioned country fare - just how she'd been raised. Seemed to give her plenty of energy and that probably was why she kept the weight off. She was always busy with this or that and really loved her life.

Mike loved the fact that she was an uncomplicated girl raised in the country. She didn't have the hang-ups that some of his previous girlfriends had had, who would worry about their hair or their figures. They spent so much time worrying about their bodies and how they looked that they missed out on simply enjoying life. So, he loved his light-hearted and fun Cassie and wouldn't trade her for any other woman in the whole world, no matter how perfectly they might be formed or done up. His Cassie was the prettiest picture to him and he loved to walk about the city with her and show off his girl. She was natural and loving and caring and she made him happy. What more could he ask for?

"Well, Cassie, it's raining!"

"So?" asked Cassie, looking at the mischievous glint in Mike's eyes.

"You should always eat pancakes for breakfast on a rainy day. That's our family tradition. I got woken up by the rain on the roof and couldn't sleep again, so decided I'd start preparing our breakfast. It's all ready to go when we get up in the morning," smiled Mike.

"Ooh... pancakes! My favourite!" said Cassie eagerly, thinking she liked this family even more if that was one of their 'traditions'.

"Come, sweet Cass," said Mike, lovingly wrapping his arm around her body, which was still warm from their cosy bed. "Let's sit and watch the rain come down. Rain is always so romantic."

Cassie had no argument with this proposal. They were both wide awake now, and there was no point in going upstairs to toss and turn trying to find their sleep with its dreams again. She decided she'd rather dream awake now, with her beloved Mike, and watch the steady downpour that was hammering happily on their tin roof.

She grabbed her old woollen blanket and they snuggled under it on the couch. Mike had pulled the curtains wide open so that they could look through the lounge window, which opened out onto their slightly wild and overgrown garden. The dim dawn light was slowly lighting up the garden as the still hidden sun spread its rays outwards, the light reaching up into this new day giving it birth.

They sat quietly, listening to the rhythm of the rain and watching the sky pour its emotion down onto the foliage outside their window. It was such a peaceful time, just before dawn and before the birds even got an idea that the new day was imminent. Mike put his giant hand around hers and they lost themselves in this moment of romantic rain.

After a long while of silently watching and listening to the rain, Cassie murmured, "Funny how the rain cries onto the plants and brings them more life. It's like the sky is letting all its feelings out and after that things can grow again. We should remember that - when we have lots of things building up inside us like clouds, we should just let it all out, even if there is some 'rain' and then we can grow again in the sun."

Mike, the practical one, looked at his little Cassie with soft and tender eyes. This is what he loved about this being. She was so poetic and sincere. It brought a whole new level to the way he viewed life. He was less than half a man without her, and together they were bigger than two. It was just how things were. They were meant for each other and they knew it and were happy to bask in the certainty that this life was meant for them to travel together.

"Cassie, you know what, I can't sleep again this morning. We're up now and the day is coming soon. I'm starting to feel really hungry. Why don't I cook up those pancakes. We can have an early breakfast to help us with our growing," said Mike, sweetly following on in his practical way from her poetry.

"Now you're talking, honey! I'm also feeling ravenous! Let's hurry and get our romantic breakfast ready!"

Within in a short while, they each had a plate piled with pancakes and syrup, sprinkled lightly with cinnamon. What a feast! They took their plates back to the couch in the lounge and ate there, on their laps. The rain carried on, almost drowning out the soft clatter of their knives and forks as they ate and satisfied their ravenous appetites. The sun was now following behind its rays, threatening any moment to peep over the horizon to the east. Daylight was entering more and more into their wild garden.

"Cass, you know I'm glad we couldn't sleep! Sleep would have robbed us of these moments. It's been fun watching the day get born."

"Yes! And the nice part is, it's Saturday and we didn't plan anything yet -

so we can decide now what we'll do with our new born day," said Cassie as she finished off her last pancake.

Well, there's something urgent I need to attend to first," said Mike.

"Then we can do what we want with our brand-new day."

"Oh?" said Cassie, a little disappointed. She thought she was going to have Mike all to herself all day today and didn't like the idea of him having to handle other matters first. "How long will that take?"

"Not too much of our time, Cass. I'll just nip upstairs to my office to get things sorted, then I'll be joining you for the rest of the day OK?"

Cassie swallowed her disappointment and nodded. She knew better than to argue if Mike had something urgent to do. She resigned herself to cuddling alone under her blanket and continued to watch the rain come pouring down.

It was not 20 minutes later, that she heard Mike descending the staircase again. "So quick?" she asked, hoping that he wasn't just coming to fetch something only to return upstairs again.

"Cass, may I come and share your blanket again and watch the rain with you?"

"Of course, Mike!"

Mike spoke gently to his dear Cassie, just loud enough to be heard against the constant rhythm of the rain. "Cass, we are so comfortable here under our blanket. We are so comfortable together in life. We both know that this is how we want to go forward. I've been saving for a rainy day, you know."

Cassie felt a surge of excitement come over her. She could sense that Mike had something up his sleeve. What could he possibly be about to suggest?

"I've saved for a moment like this and I'm not going to wait anymore," said Mike. "Close your eyes, Cass."

"Ooh - surprise!" she said, obligingly shutting her eyes tight and resisting with all her might, the urge to peek.

"Cass, I've saved for this rainy day. Now it's here - no point in waiting longer." He gently took her small hand and opened up those slender fingers. Cassie's eyes were still shut tight, as Mike took out the shiny gold ring from his pocket. It displayed a gorgeous tanzanite stone embedded amongst some tiny diamond flecks. Just as the red sun finally peeked over the horizon beyond their rampant garden, he gently placed the ring around her finger as she opened her eyes and gasped quietly.

"Will you marry me, Cassie, and journey together with me and stay at my side through this life?"

Now it was Mike who was being poetic.

"As long as you make me pancakes," smiled Cassie tenderly as she cried some soft tears of sweet happiness, along with the rain.

The End

# Romance in the Moonlight

The bright glow of an almost-full moon outshone the twinkling of her star sisters tonight. Looking up at the huge, clearly lit sky, Jade thought it looked almost like daytime. She was standing high up on the outdoor patio that she'd created on the rooftop of her house, and from this vantage point, the magnified moon looked kind and caring - as if she was smiling down on Jade tonight. It was hot - even out here on the roof - and Jade welcomed the fresh breeze that blew sporadically, tugging gently at her flimsy nightwear. Jade preferred not to use the air-con, as she liked nature's fresh air - so here she was on her roof-top, kissed by the night breeze and admiring her beautiful moon far away.

The little breeze in the night air seemed to be much stronger the higher she looked towards her magnificent moon further up in the sky. She noticed that now and again, wisps of dark clouds scudding across the moon's bright face, caused shadows to flicker on the concrete deck beneath her feet. Jade imagined being up there in that enormous wind, racing along with those clouds. This was truly a beautiful night. She didn't bother anymore about not being able to sleep in the heat. She decided to relax out here on her rooftop and enjoy being a tiny part of this glorious universe.

Sitting there in the quiet of the night, watching the dark clouds cutting into the brightness of the moon, Jade thought about recent events in her life. Her life seemed to reflect what she was observing on this beautiful night. She sometimes felt like the bright moon, capable of shining out and conquering all her challenges. But at the moment, her ability to shine was being obscured by one of those passing clouds.

Life had not always been very easy for Jade. She had entered into this lifetime in this harsh universe with more than her fair share of troubles. Orphaned at a young age due to tragic circumstances, she had spent 2 of her early years in an orphanage and was then taken on as a foster child by the kindest couple she'd ever met, to this day. Molly and Jasper Jones.

Through the years, this sweet couple had nurtured her and done their best for her. They had passed on their sound values – values that have transcended time and cultures through the ages. The universal values held and taught by most great religious leaders and philosophers. Values that outlast or complement any ebb and flow of bright ideas about how to live. She knew how to love, how to be kind and how to not judge but to rather assist her fellow man. Above all, Molly and Jasper had taught her to believe in herself and have confidence in her own viewpoints, as her view on life was based on good. And she knew that if she acted according to good, her viewpoints must be correct. This was probably one of the best gifts of all that they gave her.

The home they offered was temporary. But the seeds of emotional and spiritual strength that they planted were the gift and blessing of a lifetime and who knows, perhaps the gift of lifetimes to come. Jade was aware that she was not just a mortal, flesh and blood specimen of nature. She knew she came from somewhere and was going somewhere in this universe. And she felt that what Molly and Jasper had given her as a spiritual Being, was a priceless and eternal gift. And she cherished it.

Jade was not blind to the opportunity life had thrown at her when Molly and Jasper had crossed her path of life. All of 4 years old when she first moved in with them, she knew that she should grasp this chance and run with this ball. And thus, Jade was now an extremely successful architect in Atlanta. Her work was sought after and her buildings were fast becoming her best form of direct promotion of her incredible talent.

Jade was on her own two feet now and had a fancy home of her own, designed by herself. Her house was so stunningly beautiful that it naturally drew in new business.

Now, here she sat on her rooftop patio, feeling like a tiny speck in this magnificent universe; the moon gracing her sector of this grand scheme as she sat contemplating her present situation.

She had the perfect job, doing what she loved and never short of work. She was settled and happy but she hadn't really made it in the area of stable relationships as she'd put her efforts into focussing more on her career and financial stability.

And now, Jade was in love. She was really in love, for the first time in her life. She had been loved by those who had raised her, been admired by young guys in her teens, been flattered by men as she entered womanhood. Jade had tested the waters of romance and reached out with her own love. She'd had dates and fun times. But now, in all her 27 years of experiencing relationships of different types, she had finally welcomed into her space another being who was a kindred spirit. She knew that Alex (she called him "Al") was the person that romantics dreamed of, that poems were written about and that movies were based on, and she had no shred of doubt in her self-determined mind that Al was the man for her. Their paths had found each other in this world full of billions of people.

She sighed as she leaned back in her long, reclining patio chair and gazed up again at the moon smiling gently down on her. Another dark cloud whisked its way past the bright, golden face of her moon and Jade felt a tinge of anxiety as she thought about her situation with Al. It should have all been perfect. She'd met her soul mate. He loved her with a passion and she him.

But... Al didn't fit in with anything that her current life expected of her. Al was a Jamaican musician. To the degree that Jade was settled and financially stable, Al was footloose and fancy free, and lived a cash-in, cash-out existence. He was successful in his field and highly in demand. But his life was totally different to Jade's. Their cultures were worlds apart. But they were totally and hopelessly in love with each other. They were two souls who had a need for each other just as a thirst in the desert needs quenching. They were two beings who were raised in different parts of the world, but who found each other amongst the millions of potential partners who could have come their way.

When they had first met, that night in Kingston, where Jade was seeing a client and had taken some time out to relax at a restaurant where Al was playing a gig, they both knew it in the first moment. They both felt the energy waves from some unknown source flowing hectically between them. They felt ignited with aliveness. It was as if, together, they generated more power and thrust into the universe than apart. They could create more, do more, and be more to the world as a united couple than as two separate entities.

Just as a magnet and an electrical wire provide energy to light a whole house, this sensation of power and surging energy that they each felt in each other's presence was for them, the unmistakable physics of love for the right person. It was meant to be. It was a good fit. But the 2 parts of the whole were made in different countries. If it could work in manufacturing, with "made in Japan" uniting with "made in the UK" then Jade and Al could also make it as a combined unit "made in Jamaica" and "made in the USA".

Al, from his side, was no ordinary island man. Yes - he loved the sun, the sea and cricket. Nothing was better than going to a live match and watching Chris Gayle lop that hard cricket ball over the stands and sometimes out towards the beach. This was island life. And Al thrived on the laid-back style of living. He was never in a rush and time was about when his next gig was starting. This was just the way he was raised and it was how it had always been. Kingston was a huge place to him, but he still preferred the quieter parts of town although he did his gigs where he was needed. But Al had a mind of his own and despite his laid-back appearance he knew what he liked and what he didn't like and he was pretty determined in his own way.

He knew that Jade was the woman for him. He didn't know that just by looking at her, beautiful as she was when he first spotted her in the fading evening light at the beach restaurant. He knew it when he talked to her and got to know her during the project she was working on in the outskirts of his city. Jade was designing a dream retirement home on the coast of his island for a wealthy couple who had chosen to live in beautiful Jamaica.

During her stay there, Jade and Al made time for long walks on the beach and down the streets of Kingston. It was a romantic time and Jade enjoyed the contrast between her hectic work day with demanding clients, and the relaxed and laid-back evenings and weekend times that she and Al managed to squeeze in between his gigs and her project time.

It was during these beautiful walks, that they got to know each other as spiritual beings, devoid of the trappings of their different cultures and lifestyles. These moments afforded them time to simply communicate about deep-seated ideas they each had, their passions, their dreams. Those things were not material or based on an expected lifestyle. They were based on their individual aspirations as unique spirits wearing flesh bodies in this time in the universe.

Each had a passion for helping children to realize their dreams and improve their lives. Jade was involved in work with orphaned kids back home in Atlanta as she had always wanted to give back what she'd so luckily gained from Molly and Jeff. Al, in turn, gave music lessons to the poorer kids in the villages, who couldn't afford to pay for lessons.

Although totally different, they were so alike. Peel off the outer layer of apparency, and underneath, they were souls from the same place. During these walks and while Jade was out of her usual city environment, their relationship looked simple and inevitable. It seemed too good to be true. Jade wondered how long it would really last.

Al didn't worry about complexities. He took life as it rolled out for him. He didn't really stress about imagined problems when they hadn't arrived yet. He would handle them if they ever did arrive. Right now, one thing he was totally certain of was that he had found the woman who was right for him, and whom he wanted to love and hold. He didn't find it more complicated than that.

On the last night before Jade needed to return to Atlanta, they walked for a very long way along the beach. They got to their favourite spot where they liked to sit on the sand and look out over the water. The yellow moon was staring down at them and in her soft light the palm trees cast long shadows on the sand.

Jade didn't want this moment to end, ever. She sat quietly next to Al. He took hold of her hand, so gently. He was a huge man and she felt so comfortable and at peace having him at her side. After all their long talks about their passions and their dreams, there seemed nothing more to say. They knew they had to be together. That was the simple part. But Jade just didn't see how.

Sitting there silently next to her love, the tears started to roll gently yet uncontrollably down her cheeks. A deep and disturbing sensation rose up in her and she felt lost and out of control for the first time since she'd been taken in by her foster parents, all those years ago. All the morale boosting and confidence building that she'd gained in those lovely years with Molly and Jeff had not prepared her for a biting moment like this. She felt the loss all over again that she'd experienced, young as she was, when she'd been separated from her birth parents. She didn't even know these feelings were still there, harboured below the surface of her successful life. But now, with the potential threat of losing this giant man sitting next to her, whom she loved with all her heart, the sting of that distant pain seared through her body and senses and she sobbed and sobbed until the sand was wet.

Al knew what was happening. He knew her story. He didn't say a word. He just closed his giant hand a little tighter around her delicate, artist's fingers and sat quietly as she sobbed. He allowed her to let the dam spill out onto the moon-bathed sand and waited.

Finally, Jade's grief subsided and she leaned closer to him and rested her head on his shoulder. They continued to stare out over the water and at the yellow-gold moon.

"Al, I need to go home to Atlanta. You know that," she said softly. "I'll miss you. We'll work it out. I don't know how, but we'll work it out."

"I know," said Al. "You see our moon there? It's our moon. When you see it in Atlanta, I'll be seeing it here and I'll have you here in spirit."

"Al, every time I see the moon, I'll be with you," she whispered. "But you can also come sometime and see our moon in

Atlanta. I can't pull you off your island. I know you are happy living here. I'm not sure what we can do. I like Atlanta. We have to work things out."

"I know," he said. "Let's walk. Things are going to work out."

They walked off, arm in arm across the beach and up towards her hotel. They enjoyed the moment and Jade pushed the future out of her mind. She was learning from Al how to go with the flow of the moment and have the "now". There was a freedom in that and a new way to experience life. There was a difference between planning and taking responsibility for the future, and just plain old worrying for no reason. They trusted in their love and the decisions they had made together and enjoyed the last walk before her return to Atlanta.

Now, here was Jade on her roof top, seeing their moon. The dark clouds coming across, followed by the brisk wind blowing them swiftly off her moon's face so that she shone brightly again. When Jade thought about the problems of creating her life together with Al, she felt the brightness of her life going into shadow, like the moon behind the clouds. She started to see the clouds building up and gathering mass. Now they were practically closing off her romantic moon's shiny face.

She resolved to do something. Her life couldn't go on like this, at the effect of distance and cultures. Surely, with their energy that they ignited exponentially in each other, she and Al could work something out. He seemed so laid-back. He had assured her that it would all be fine. He seemed to just roll along with it and had a sense of knowing that things would work out. But she was from a different world. In her world, she felt she needed to act, to do something, to plan and make something happen. He seemed to be like the breeze blowing her nightie - just flow and it's going to all be fine.

She lay back on her long deck chair and closed her eyes to the darkening clouds. Her moon had almost disappeared. She didn't like to see that. Before she knew it, she had dozed off and then fell into a deep sleep. The next thing she was aware of was the twittering of the birds starting up in her garden.

Becoming aware that she was not sleeping in her usual bed, Jade opened her eyes briefly in her comfortable reclining chair and took in the beautiful space she had created at the top of her roof. From here, everything looked fresh and green. She was in the sky, looking down on some of the smaller trees in her garden. Even some of the birds' homes were lower down than her vantage point, here at the top of her house. She closed her eyes again and rolled over, determined to get in another little snooze out here in the fresh, morning breeze. It was really early, and she hadn't realized what a wonderful place the roof top was to spend the night. The day would only officially start in a couple of hours, so she settled back into her slumber.

But there was a shrill sound that rose above the birds and which penetrated even their incessant chatter. Slowly, in her half-asleep state, Jade began to realize that it was her phone ringing in her bedroom below. This was an odd time for her phone to ring and she felt her heart start to beat rapidly as anxiety set in. She wasn't expecting a call at such an odd time.

Scurrying rapidly down the stairs leading from the roof-top into the landing outside her bedroom, she hoped she'd get to the phone in time. But just as she got to her bedroom door, it rang off. This was most annoying. Her fresh-air sleep had been rudely interrupted. Hastily picking up her phone, she saw Al's number reflecting as the missed call. This was strange. He wouldn't ordinarily call so early in the morning. Her mind started to race as she tried to make sense of this. Then she spotted the 3 missed calls from last night - she must have not heard them as she'd slept so soundly up on her roof. At first, she hesitated, too nervous to phone back, not knowing what to expect. Her fingers froze as she hovered in hesitation before pressing on the gorgeous photo she had next to his phone details on her shiny phone screen. Finally, she touched it as lovingly as if it were his skin, and listened tentatively as it rang briefly before he picked up.

"Jade, I'm so sorry to call you so early! I did try 3 times last night when I thought you'd still be awake."

"Al, I'm sorry I didn't hear your calls! What's going on?" she asked, breathing fast and trying to keep calm.

"Atlanta girl, it's all good, it's good news. Relax sweet girl."

Jade could hear the smile in his voice and saw that array of sparkling white teeth in her mind's eye as he spoke these reassuring words. She sat down on her bed and took a deep breath.

"So what's such good news, Al, that you work me up at 5 a.m. to hear?" she asked playfully.

"I told you things are gonna work out for us. We had a moon last night - did you see it?"

"Yes - our moon! It was bright last night, but then the clouds came over. How did it look in Kingston?" asked Jade

"That, I can't tell you sweet Atlanta girl, because I'm in Atlanta! I got a gig in a hotel downtown. A six-month gig. I'm here to be with my sweet Atlanta girl, if you'll let me in."

"Where are you, Al? Of course you can come through. That is so exciting!"

"I'm right here Baby, outside your house. I couldn't sleep, knowing I was so close to you. It was supposed to be a civilized surprise later in the day. But you know I don't do "civilized" all that well."

Jade rushed down to the front door and hurriedly opened the locks, not bothering to listen further on the phone. She threw the door open and there he was, her giant Jamaican, filling up the doorway and smiling that glistening, white smile of sparkling teeth, from ear to ear.

She gasped in excitement and fell into his huge arms. He held her close for some minutes before she thought to invite him inside. Finally, they made their way through to the lounge where they sat together on the long, soft couch, taking each other in.

"You know, I go the way the wind blows and I dance to the rhythms that life gives me. Life gave me you, sweet Jade, and we're going to work this out because we have each other. I like your city. I can live in it for 6 months. And since that stunning beach-front house that you designed was completed, there are so many people asking for you to design their buildings. You'll have plenty of work in Kingston. We are who we are. We walk on our path and dance in the moonlight to our own songs. We don't have to worry about what other people say we should or shouldn't do. This is our journey, our voyage through this life. Let's do it, Atlanta girl," he said to her while holding tightly around her hand.

Jade thought back to that night on the beach as he held her hand. There was no turning back now. She was not going to leave again for another city without him. He was right. This was their journey for them to take on their own agreed-upon terms.

"Let's do it, Atlanta Love. And you can call me your Kingston Girl," murmured Jade, softly, in the morning light.

The End

# Romance at the Fireside

Jenna gazed quietly into the roaring, crackling fire in the old lounge. She had a long weekend off from college and had come out to her favourite hide-away mountain cabin for some own time up in the fresh, healthy mountain air. It was winter and tonight Jenna was enjoying a cozy evening protected from the outside elements, while the wind whirled and howled around the log home. The cabin was old and full of creaks and moans - especially in this type of weather - and the window shutters rattled in protest with each new gust of whining wind.

But Jenna was focussed on the even louder sound of her blazing, bright, red and orange fire. As a young child she'd come up to this cabin with her parents on many a winter's holiday and this was still her sanctuary from the noise of busy life in the modern world. Some of her college friends had thought she was totally crazy to be coming up to this lonely hut on her own, but Jenna thought they were equally crazy to be staying back in the big city with all its traps and snares. She had been looking forward to this long weekend on her own for some time and she was thoroughly indulging herself in pleasure on her first night in front of her fire.

With plenty of books and plenty of provisions of food, Jenna was quite content to while away her few days off here in the mountains before returning to college to start working on her new term's assignment. Her boyfriend, Tim, was inundated with work at the office. He'd left college the year before and was in the process of passionately proving himself to the boss and colleagues in his first year out in the world of finance, stocks, shares and ... yes... snares. Well, that was Jenna's feeling anyway. However, Tim had worked out that he could come up to spend some time with her in the cabin on Sunday and she looked forward to that.

As this was her final year at college, she had also wanted some time to herself to think about her future and where she really wanted to go. Her Mom had unfortunately passed on a year ago and her Dad, since her parents' divorce when she was sixteen, had moved to Dubai for a lucrative business deal. She hadn't seen him for a while and wasn't particularly close to her Dad. He seemed happy enough but was no longer really in close or regular contact and had chased the buck to keep himself satisfied with life.

Jenna was different. Her Mom had been an artist. She had never worked in an office or climbed the corporate ladder, or made efforts to impress anyone with her business skills. She just painted, and sold her paintings. Some months she sold lots and some months they had to tighten their belts. But since her father had left, Jenna had never starved and life always seemed to smile on her and her Mom as they followed their natural impulses towards the things that made them happy. Being an only child, Jenna had grown very close to her Mom over the years. But Mom wasn't here now to chat to and Jenna needed to think things through on her own and plan for her future.

Jenna was at college on a bursary and Mom had left a bit of money for her, but that would run out soon and Jenna was now faced with the challenges of making it in a modern world where, whether one liked it or not, the buck did matter to some degree. She realized she couldn't just live in a dream world of reading novels and staring into relaxing fires. She had to make something of her life.

She knew that Tim was going to make it financially. He was a go-getter and business and commerce were his natural inclination. He loved the fast pace of his job and having to make crucial decisions in a split second to ensure that the profits landed in the right spot. In fact, he thrived on it. Jenna was totally different, but she loved Tim. So they would need to work things out or go their separate ways at some point if their chosen avenues became too disparate. On the other hand, the idea of marrying Mr. Money was also a little tempting, as that could solve a lot of things... or could it?

So Jenna sat in the threadbare old chair that had occupied this prime spot near the fire for 2 generations, and contemplated her future. She had to make her own mind up on things. Her Mom was gone and she was, apart from Tim, basically alone in this world. What she did know, is that she had a burning purpose to help people and wanted to travel and meet people from different countries. As she felt that education was the key to whatever a person wanted to achieve in life, she had decided she would combine her college English degree with teaching. There must be a way to marry the travelling with the teaching. But then that did not leave much room for marrying Tim.

As she stared into the fire, she started to feel quite lucky. Here she was at the start of her adult life with the luxury of being able to paint her own canvas of the future. Perhaps her future was going to be a little like this fire. You start it up with the strike of a match, and then it burns brightly but one can't always predict which flame will take where. One also has no idea when exactly the fire will die down to its last embers and breathe its last breath of oxygen. But what she could predict is that her life would burn with her passions as long as she breathed life into them. And that's the one big, overriding conclusion she came to that night.

She knew she didn't want to just work for money and then buy things she felt she should have because her friends had them. Perhaps because her Mom had shown her a different way to live, Jenna was comfortable with her own needs and desires for the future. She knew that she had certain passions as an individual and unless she could weave those into her life as part of her career, or as part of her leisure time, her life would not burn brightly like the fire in front of her. She also knew that it was entirely up to her to light her own fires in life and burn her own path forward. What she decided at quiet times like this would carry forward if she guided and controlled her actions in the direction she wanted them to go. It was up to her to create her future how she wanted it to be. She needed to decide where to light her fires and light them. And she was in charge of keeping them burning as long as she wanted them to be alive and active and hot.

Feeling pretty smug at her own personal philosophical discovery, Jenna got ready for bed. She looked forward to falling asleep to the sounds of the wind. She always felt so safe and snug up here in the family cabin and slept like a log whenever she came up here.

Jenna spent Saturday cleaning up the cabin, which had been unoccupied for some months. Later that day she put on her huge, warm duffel coat and braved the icy wind to take a short walk in the woods. As it was winter, all the trees appeared stark and semi frozen and it was easier to find the old paths than when everything was overgrown in the summer months. She walked and walked, enjoying the invigorating air and finally turned back before it got too dark. She stopped briefly at the outside store room to collect some more firewood for tonight's crackling blaze.

When she got in, she saw that her phone was flashing with 3 messages. She'd decided that even though it was supposed to be a retreat weekend, she would still bring her mobile phone in case anyone needed to contact her. When she looked, all the messages were from Tim. He'd left 3 messages asking her to call him. The last one sounded pretty desperate and intense, and Jenna was alarmed at the tone in Tim's voice.

She called him immediately.

"Jen? Thank goodness you called! I was getting so worried about you alone there in the woods, especially when you didn't return my calls!"

"Sorry Tim, I was out for a walk. What's up?" replied Jenna, anxious at the sound of Tim's stressed voice.

"Jen, I called you because I need to come and talk to you. This can't wait. I took a chance and drove up to the little hotel half an hour away. Can I come through now? I know it's getting late, Jen, but I really, really, urgently need to talk to you."

Jenna's heart sank. This sounded bad. She had been looking forward to another solitary evening enjoying her books and enjoying sitting in front of the fire alone. This is how Jenna was. She didn't really fit in with the other college students who liked loud parties and experimenting with drugs and alcohol. She had long since accepted that she was different and was surprised that Tim had even been interested in dating her because usually the loud and partying type of girls got the successful guys. But this was Tim, her boyfriend of over 6 months, asking if he could come and talk to her. He'd already driven for an hour hoping that she'd receive him. She couldn't exactly turn him down.

"Sure, Tim. Come on through," said Jenna, keen to see him now and find out what all the fuss was about, that he couldn't even discuss on the phone. It was clearly important enough to pull him out of his work project earlier than planned as he was only due to come through tomorrow at lunch time.

Sometime later, just as the wind started up again with another night storm, she heard Tim's sports car slowly negotiating the dirt road leading up to the cabin. Not the ideal transport for this kind of journey, Jenna thought - but that was Tim - her city go-getting boyfriend. She smiled at the ludicrous situation she found herself in. But love was one of those unpredictable flames in the main fire that just starts up from a little twig somewhere unpredicted and burns brightly, sometimes for a short while and sometimes for a lifetime until the whole fire dies. She didn't know what kind of love she'd found here. She was too young and inexperienced. She just knew that right now, as she heard him jogging up towards the cabin, that she loved him.

She'd opened the door before he could get there to knock. "Come in quickly Tim, the wind is coming up. It gets pretty fierce out there at this time of the year."

In a flash, Tim was through the door which Jenna closed and locked firmly, closing out the blast of icy air that had entered along with Tim.

"Hi Jen, thank you so much for letting me come through earlier! I know this was not the plan. I just had to see you!"

"OK Tim, take it easy. Let's have some soup and warm you up, then let's light the fire and chat. It sounds so urgent - but let's settle down first so that you can relax - we have all evening to chat.

This moment was oh so typical of their relationship. Tim always rushing around and Jenna usually calm and laid-back, taking her time to logically process what was occurring. Again, she wondered how this could be that 2 such different personalities had found themselves so attracted to each other - like super-strong magnets that couldn't easily be pried apart.

Jenna smiled up at this gorgeous guy in the dull light of the gas lamp. He looked even more handsome than usual, standing here in the peace and tranquillity of the rustic log cabin. His hair was a mess of curls and his face was flushed with the fast jog he'd just done from his shiny sports car into this very basic mountain home. "Slow down, Tim, you're here now. There's no rushing in this place." Jenna looked adoringly up at that earnest face. She loved this man so much that she sometimes ached with the intensity of her emotion. He reached out with his icy cold hands and gently held her face in them before leaning forward to kiss her.

It was at sweet moments like this that Jenna's grand philosophy took a knock. All the logical thinking she'd done the night before melted into a moment of pure passion as she and Tim lost themselves in their loving embrace. This was incredibly romantic. They were up here alone in a mountain cabin. There was no-one else anywhere in sight. The only neighbours were the rabbits and deer in their winter hidey holes outside in the dark and stormy night.

Finally, after a hearty soup and bread, they lit the fire and settled down to talk.

"Jen, something's come up at work. It is going to affect us big time and I've been so stressed about it because I just don't know what to do. You and I are so good together and I don't want work to come between us, but I have a career to build too. I just don't know what to do and I don't want to hurt you. I'm so confused," Tim blurted out.

Jenna was astonished. This was not the Tim she knew. Tim was usually so certain of himself, certain of his career moves and where he was going and what he wanted. She hadn't known him like this. Usually she was the one that went into confusions about where she was headed in life. But at the same time, what he was implying wasn't lost on her. This could be the end of the road for the two of them. She went onto full alert, waiting for him to spit out what he needed to say.

"I've been selected for a contract in India. It's a big deal Jen, I haven't accepted yet because of us. I needed to talk to you. It would mean I'll be away for 2 years in India manning up the new branch we're opening up there. It's exciting Jen, but I don't know if I should take it."

Jenna looked at this man she adored more than anyone else in the world. It was the first time in their relationship that she'd seen him so distressed and scattered in his thoughts.

"Tim, look at the fire - do you see those flames leaping all about?" said Jenna quietly to Tim. She wanted to get him to focus his thoughts on something outside of his scrambled mind. "Let's just enjoy the crackling fire and the flames - look how they come from nowhere and go to nowhere - and all in a fabulous array of orange, yellow and red." She reached her hand out to Tim's and held his hand firmly in hers to steady him. "Listen to that howling wind outside! We are so cozy and snug here and we don't need to worry about flying to India just yet. Let's enjoy our time now because you're here and I'm here and this is bonus time for us."

Tim started to relax and calm down. Jenna approached life so differently. He couldn't believe how calmly she was taking this news. He had thought she'd be so mad at him for even considering leaving her while he chased after his career half-way across the planet in a strange country.

They sat together watching the flames grow and disappear, then re-form and grow again. The wind kept up its gloomy wailing in the cold winter night outside and as the two of them sat quietly holding hands, it felt as if time had ceased to exist in this solitary cabin up in the mountain.

Eventually Tim spoke. "You're not mad at me, Jen?"

"How could I be mad at you, Tim? We are both young. We've been dating 6 months - you have your dreams and your goals to follow. You need to work out what's the right thing to do for you, your job, for me. I'm glad you came to talk to me."

"Jen, I don't see how I can leave you but I also can't pass up this opportunity. It's been tearing me apart and that's why I had to come up and talk about this. It's going to be so different. I probably won't even make as much money to begin with, but it's a challenge and an adventure - and it's a chance for me to spread my wings and see what I can achieve. Plus, I'll be helping so many people to uplift their lives. I really want to see if I can pull this off. I don't know if you'll really even want me as your boyfriend - I won't be driving a sporty car or taking you to fancy parties in the city, that's for sure!"

Jenna felt a surge of excitement as she began to realize that Tim was a whole lot more than the man she already loved. She saw, for the first time, a side to Tim that had not revealed itself so clearly before. He was not like her Dad, just chasing the buck. Tim too, had a burning purpose and it was not driven by the buck. She understood that Tim, too, wanted to light his own fires and keep them burning the way he wanted them to burn.

"Oh Tim!" Jenna tightened her grasp around his huge hand. "Do you really think I care about what car you drive, or parties in the city? Look at where we are right now! I'm happy to simply be with you in this old wooden log cabin with no electricity and just a fire burning. I want you to be happy following your dreams. I have dreams too, Tim, I have been thinking about those. They definitely don't include sports cars and fancy parties!"

"But Jenna, I'll be away for 2 years. I don't want to lose you, but I can't hold onto you if I'm going away. I can't force you to wait for me. I can't choose between you and my career - I just don't know what to do." Tim started to get agitated again and Jenna got up silently and put another 2 logs onto the fire to make sure it kept up its pace of crackling, burning heat and colour.

"Tim, you don't need to choose. If you want me at your side, if you truly do, I'll join you. I've always wanted to travel. I've always wanted to help people and work with education. I have one more final practical assignment to do at college. I don't see why I can't do that in India! There must be lots of kids who want to learn to speak English over there."

The freshly loaded logs caught in the big fire and ignited with a rush of flames and heat as Jenna spoke.

They held hands again and were quiet, listening to the crackling and roaring of the freshly fed fire. Both of them had ignited their own passions this evening, in front of this cozy fire. They were like the 2 logs with freshly kindled purpose, burning together brightly into the dark night.

They both knew in this instant that they were in control of their own burning purposes in their lives. And they didn't need to chase money or parties or fast cars. They simply needed to keep putting fresh logs onto the warm and passionate fires that burned in their own hearts. They needed to stay true to their own worlds and didn't need to join in the smoky smog of a rat-race of artificial values and expectations. In that moment in front of the fire, Jenna and Tim knew they were going to make it together as a couple in this pressured modern world.

The End

# Romantic Road

Lara stood at the top of the long road that wound around towards the subway which was out of view. This was the road she and her childhood friends had walked, skipped and run down depending on which direction they were going to and from school.

It was always an exciting moment if they happened to be walking through the subway just as the huge train came pounding and rattling across the bridge above them. It was a lucky sign. The tale went that if you were walking with a boy at that moment, he would be the next one to kiss you. This was why it was named the "Romantic Road".

Now it was 2 decades later and Lara was visiting her parents at her childhood home, enjoying some fond memories of older times and thinking about the very bumpy romantic road of life she'd recently travelled. She'd learned from the great teacher - Life itself - that romance took more than walking down a road by that name. One needed to carve one's own path of romance, and not rely on "luck" but really work at it and create that path constantly if one wanted things to work out.

The country road Lara stared at now had remained unchanged by time. Caressed by the brisk breezes coming over the majestic Drakensberg Mountains, the foliage near the road always had some treasured surprises, no matter the season. The little miniature yellow daisies that thrust their sunny heads up through the lush green grass on either side of the romantic road had replaced themselves over and over during the years that had passed. But today they looked as if time had stood still - same daisies, same grass, same smells of pollen and damp evening dew.

She watched as the yellow sun started painting the sky red as it sank slowly beyond the faraway hills. This had always been her favourite time of the day, when everything started settling down - following the example of the sun. There was still enough light to see the countryside but it had a soft and gentle sensation to it and even the harsh-sounding Hadeda Ibis birds toned down their call as the evening came to meet the red sky.

Turning back towards the family house, she picked a few yellow daisies who had now closed their petals to go to sleep. They were like miniature golden suns that had closed down for the day. She strolled back down the road, through the rickety gate around her parents' home and up the path to the big old oak door.

The evening was spent relaxing with her parents and younger brother and catching up on news. Lara now lived a 4 hour drive away and didn't have lots of opportunities to visit. So the family savoured these times when she was back in town. It was always good for all of them to have Lara back. She put the daisies she'd picked into a glass of water on the table in her bedroom - they would catch the morning sun and open their petals to welcome the next day.

All too soon, it was time to head back to the city and after some brief "goodbyes", which Lara hated, she was on the highway headed back home. This was a strange idea to Lara, that she now thought she was heading home when she was leaving her childhood and family home and heading for the city. But things change over time and Lara just wasn't comfortable any longer in this little village she grew up in. It was good for a short visit but then she would get restless and want to get back to the city and her fast-paced career in advertising, which she absolutely loved.

Besides this, Lara had found a new love in the city and he was definitely not a country type. She had met Gavin at an advertising convention which she had attended as a delegate from her company. Gavin was involved in photography and it seemed destined that their paths should cross. Although it had seemed like "love at first sight", Lara was cautious and didn't rush into things. She'd fairly recently come out of a long relationship with her high-school sweetheart, Mark and was definitely not going to put herself into a position to be hurt like that again in a hurry. She was so careful with this new man, that she hadn't even dared mention him to her family, who were still recovering from the disappointment of the break-up of her previous relationship.

Mark was, in the family's view, the ideal partner for Lara. He had been "Mr. Right". He came from the same background, grew up in the same village and had moved to the same city. Her parents had assumed that they would marry, give them grandchildren and life would all be peachy. But things didn't work out for either Lara or Mark - even though they'd kissed under the passing train over the bridge many times. The "luck" wore out for them. Lara had come to realize that love and sharing one's life with someone took more than a passing train superstition to make things work. She also felt heart sore at her parents' loss when she and Mark parted ways, but she couldn't go into something for the rest of her life that simply didn't feel right for her, let alone Mark. Much as she loved her family, Lara had a sense of personal integrity that didn't stretch into that sort of compromise of doing the "right" thing for the majority when it was not the right thing for her. There was no doubt for her she and Mark had made the correct decision in calling it off, even if it temporarily broke some hearts.

Gavin proved to be patient enough with her as she worked her way through her fears and other emotions associated with starting afresh in the department of love. He didn't rush her but he really did adore her and didn't hide the fact.

As they were both very committed to their careers, time together had to be planned and was always precious. The weeks flew by as they each worked their hearts out on different deadlines. Pressures mounted as the year drew to a close and ads needed to be ready for the Christmas and year-end markets. They were both exhausted and looked forward to a 2 week break when their companies would be closed for the holiday season.

They hadn't given much thought to what they would do with this time off and most places were fully booked by the time they had an evening together to chat about options. Lara was quite happy to mill around at home and relax, just as long as she could pop down to visit her family for a night or two as this would be expected at this time of the year. Gavin's parents lived overseas and so it was just 'phone-calls that were expected of him. Lara felt it would be better that she visited her family alone as she was still reticent about introducing Gavin as her boyfriend. The truth was, she was so madly in love with him, she couldn't bear the thought of something going wrong with this relationship and hurting her and her family all over again.

Although Gavin understood the loss Lara had undergone, he also didn't want to forever be linked in Lara's mind to the one that didn't work out. He had no doubts about this relationship. Lara was everything he'd ever desired in a woman and a soul mate. She and he shared the same values, things were simple when they were together. They each respected the other's careers and work ethic and communication between them was easy. Why would he need to look somewhere else or suspect it might not work when he had his ideal mate right in front of his eyes? But things weren't so simple for Lara and he knew she had to go through what she had to go through and was willing to stay the course and give her the time to work through it. He knew it would be worth the persistence.

So they sat down for the evening after enjoying a simple supper together and chatted about the 2 precious weeks that were coming up and how they should use the time for maximum benefit all round.

Understanding Lara's predicament to some degree, although keen to meet her parents, Gavin agreed that Lara should see her family over a couple of days and at least break the news to them that she had met someone else. For Lara, this was acceptable as it would not put too much hope there and then set them up for another disappointment. She realized this was so unfair on Gavin to think this way when it was clear that he doted on her and had no thoughts whatsoever of the relationship ever failing. She also knew that she'd have to change this mind-set if she was going to succeed this time in love, as it introduced negativity into the relationship that was nonsensical considering the current set of circumstances. But fortunately for her, Gavin was the philosophical sort and did grant her the time to get over this.

After her two days visit to her family, she would meet up with Gavin in a rustic hotel in the mountains and they'd spend some time together there. Gavin hoped that this would give them both the time they needed to move to the next level in their relationship. He knew what he wanted. He wanted Lara to be at his side through the rest of his living days. He wanted her to bear their children and walk the same road together through whatever life brought to them - good or bad. For him, it was very simple. She was his ideal partner to walk the road of life at his side. He just needed her to catch up with him and embrace this and he thought that spending some real quality time together in a tranquil setting would assist the process of bringing her to see this simplicity too.

And so she went off with her little car packed with some Christmas goodies for the family and enough clothes for the second part of her trip with Gavin. Lara had a surprise for her parents. She had been saving for some years since leaving university to pay back the money they had paid in for her to study. They never asked her for this, but gave it from their own hard-earned cash, which had not come easy for them but they always did their best for their children. Lara had finally got the whole sum together and planned to pop this into her dad's bank account before he could refuse. She smiled quietly to herself thinking of the joy she would give and how happy she felt that she could do this for them.

Gavin waved as she drove off until he couldn't see the tiny red car anymore. He turned his attention to wrapping up some loose ends on his final work project for the year. He would leave in a couple of days for the place in the mountains, and Lara would drive there from her family's house.

The couple of days spent with her family was relaxing and rejuvenating for Lara. She always loved to see the old town where she'd grown up. She once again visited the romantic road and watched a couple of trains pass over the bridge. The daisies were still cheerfully doing sentry duty at each side of the road, and the same old sun continued to do its daily job of brightening the sky, then painting it into dusk.

She did tell them about a relationship starting and they had listened without judgment although a tad anxiously. Their anxiety was for Lara - they didn't want her to be hurt again. She also timed the moment perfectly to let them know about the fairly substantial amount of money she'd paid into her dad's account and after some small objection, there was acceptance of the gift and celebrations all round.

All too soon for her parents, it was time for her to leave for the little place Gavin had booked for them, an hour's drive away. Because she didn't let them know how far the relationship with Gavin had already developed, she mentioned nothing of the next phase of her holiday plans - they simply assumed she was heading back to the city after her visit as she usually had a lot of activities planned with her new friends - especially when she had a bit of time off from work.

So after another fond goodbye to loved ones, Lara set off again in her little red car with her parents and brother waving until she disappeared around a corner.

She arrived at the destination in the mountains a little ahead of Gavin, who'd had a longer drive. It was absolutely beautiful! This was a place of paradise - and she thought how clever Gavin had been to suggest it as it was really a good setting for romance. The hotel consisted of a main section for meals and about fifteen separate little thatched chalets which were of different sizes, for sleeping accommodation. The chalet booked for Gavin and Lara had its own private garden and the view of the mountains beyond was glorious. They towered majestically up into the bright blue sky and one had the sense one could almost touch them. Lara sat outside on a little bench in the garden and took in their grand beauty. A brisk breeze played with the wild flowers in the little garden and she breathed in deeply, enjoying the fresh mountain air.

Dozing off for a second, she was startled by the jiggling of the door lock as Gavin arrived. He gasped with delight when he saw the lovely setting for their romantic stay. He knew he'd made the right decision to bring his love here. Now he could go into high gear on creating this relationship and helping her to get her confidence up to commit to walking a new romantic path with him.

They embraced warmly and stood together on the little patio of the garden, holding hands tightly and taking in the magnificence of these powerful structures carved out by oceans of long ago. Although huge and awesome, they were not threatening, but seemed to smile down on the happy couple. Lara felt a sense of complete peace for the first time since her breakup with Mark.

The next few days were spent sleeping late, taking long walks and eating sumptuous meals in the hotel dining room, which had huge glass doors opening out to the view of the mountains. The omnipresent mountains seemed to guard over the patrons of the hotel - always silently and reliably there. Even during the most raging, thunderous summer storm that crashed through the sky on their second day, the mountains just stood there, rising up firmly in their own space, unmoved by the chaos of nature around them.

After the big storm Gavin took Lara outside onto the patio to view the wonderful rainbow that had sprung up into the freshly washed sky. He pointed out the rainbow and the mountains. "The rainbows come and go," he said softy. "But you and I are like the mountains. This relationship will last. It will not crumple under life's storms. It's up to us to hold it firm and keep walking together on the road. I know about your romantic road and how it crumpled beneath your feet. I know that the luck ran out from the kiss under the passing train. But now it's up to us to create our luck, together. We can carve our own road, together. We don't have to wait for fate. We can create our own happy future. You and I."

Lara thought it over and she knew Gavin was right. For the first time since Mark, she was feeling at peace with herself again and getting her confidence back. She wished she could fully embrace the moment and tried her best. Although quite headstrong and independent, she still felt a pull towards her family and what they expected of her. Mark had been so ideal and fitted in so well with everyone, coming from the same background. Gavin was different. He came from a different upbringing although they shared common values and passions in life. But she wanted to be extra, extra certain this time. She knew this was so unfair of her and tried to stifle these doubts and uncertainties but Gavin already knew what was whirling through her mind, like the storm of minutes before.

Unbelievably, he didn't blame her or lose his cool. He simply sat quietly with her on the patio, putting his hand on hers and let her watch the rainbow in the sky and the steam coming off the ground as the sun caught the wet grass after the downpour. He was ridiculously patient with her. She was amazed that men like this actually existed, and she felt quite embarrassed at herself for not being able to see it as simply as he did. They sat for a while, not speaking, just absorbing the moment. And then she said she needed to take a walk on her own. Gavin didn't object. He allowed her this time and watched as she strolled away down the path from the hotel towards one of the tranquil hiking trails. She needed to walk her own road right at this moment and he granted her that.

He turned his attention to what he would do with this time he had on his hands and decided to make use of the all-day coffee bar at the hotel. He'd brought along some magazines to study as part of his work projects for the coming year and this was an ideal time for him to spend on this. His business plans were short-lived, however, as the coffee shop was a friendly place and the natural thing folks did who were relaxed and on holiday was to start chatting. He met a young family and a retired couple and they all exchanged pleasantries about the beautiful location they were mutually enjoying, the recent huge storm and the incredible way the African sun made its way back to command the weather after being overpowered temporarily by the clouds and rain. He decided he was going to follow that example and keep strong in his resolve to win Lara, despite the emotional weather she was still clearly moving through. He particularly liked the retired couple, Bob and Jill. They seemed like good-hearted, wholesome people and they all had a good time whiling away some of the afternoon, which had turned pleasantly sunny.

After about an hour, Gavin started to have attention on Lara as she'd been gone for some time, so he excused himself and made off in the same direction he'd seen her walk. Anxiety set in as he didn't see any sign of her returning. He started walking more briskly along the path he had seen her take. Hearing a twig snapping around a corner ahead of him, he slowed suddenly and walked more quietly. He came from a big city where one was always constantly alert and his city instincts came flooding in. Then suddenly he saw her, bending over relaxedly, picking some little yellow daisies along the sides of the path. He ran to her in relief and swung her off her feet in exhilaration. This was his love, he wanted her so much and he would just keep at it until she could accept him unconditionally too. They embraced joyfully, as Lara clung to her daisies. She was happy and at ease. The walk had done her good. And she walked back contentedly with him, arm in arm.

Back in the hotel room, the daisies had closed their sunny faces being out of the light. She put them in a glass of water close to the sunny window sill in the bathroom so that they could greet the next day. They spent the rest of the day reading and chatting, ordered room service so that they could just be together for their evening meal, and spent a cozy night loving each other up in the fresh mountain air.

The next day as Lara was brushing her teeth, she saw that the daisies had opened up wide to the sunshine. She knew this was going to be a good day. The daisies were starting anew and she felt it was time for her to do the same thing. She'd spent a lot of time thinking on her long walk the day before and had made up her mind that she would stop being so stuck in her own needs and would give Gavin a proper chance. After all, it was not Gavin's fault that Mark had preceded him. It was so unfair of her to bring all that baggage into this beautiful budding relationship. She had resolved to make life easier for Gavin and take him for who he was and for herself, not for what her parents expected in a partner. If things went further, then she was sure they would like him. After all, if they were to get married, he would be marrying her, not her family.

So with a light heart, she got ready to go with her sweetheart to breakfast. She planned to tell him on their morning walk that she agreed with him - they were to be the strong and steadfast mountains and stay true, carving out their own romantic road through life together. She had even decided to ask if he would be willing to drive back home on their last day via her family home, which was only an hour away. It was time to break the news to her parents. She was getting more and more confident that this time she was not about to enter into something that was going to hurt and disappoint them again.

With these thoughts going through her mind, she held his hand as they entered the hotel coffee shop where the breakfasts were served. They headed for their favourite table that caught the morning sun. They both had good appetites in the fresh, rarefied mountain air and always looked forward to the hearty farm breakfasts served here. As the waiter came to pour their tea, Gavin looked over her shoulder and waved in greeting to someone, his eyes lighting up in excitement.

Lara's heart sank - she thought Gavin had perhaps met some beautiful girl at the hotel during the time she'd gone on her walk - perhaps she'd left it too late to tell him her inner-most thoughts. She felt a mild panic set in and looked at him frantically. This all happened in a split second.

"Who are you waving to?" she asked nervously, not wanting to turn around.

"Oh, some really nice people I met at the coffee shop yesterday while you were out on your walk. I'll introduce you."

Lara turned around in her chair to see Bob and Jill, who stared in disbelief. "Lara!" they exclaimed in unison.

"Mom, Dad! What are you doing here?" asked Lara in astonishment.

"Lara love," said Jill. "You so kindly paid us back your study money and we decided to use some of it for a treat. Bob brought us here yesterday for a couple of nights in the mountains. And what a lovely man you have met!  We met Gavin yesterday in the coffee bar. Good choice! "

Lara smiled quietly. The romantic road had its foundations and she and Gavin were off to a good start.


The End

# Love in the Office

Lesley hurried down the steps of the grey building she'd just been inside. She'd had her final meeting with the adoption agency that was working on her quest to locate her natural mother and brother. This had been a dream of many years. Ever since she was told by her adoptive mother at the age of 6 that she had a "real" mother and brother somewhere in the world, she'd had a yearning to meet them and re-establish the connection. She didn't really want to know more about the circumstances of her adoption. It was enough to know that her natural mother had run into hard times after the birth of her second child and could cope with keeping her brother, but had decided that Lesley would have a better chance in life under the circumstances if she were adopted. Lesley had only been with her natural mother for an hour or so after the birth, and then was passed on to her adoptive parents. She'd enjoyed a carefree upbringing with them, and they showered her with love and everything that she could wish for in terms of material needs and education.

The meeting was set for 1 month's time. She had marked the date carefully in her calendar, and the location - which would be at an outdoor café in a park not too far from her apartment. She had discovered that her natural mother lived in the same city, but that her brother had moved away and he would be in town on business at that time, so it worked out perfectly for a family reunion.

Putting all of this out of her mind now, as the date and location was settled, Lesley turned her thoughts to other things.

She had been a highly successful computer programmer, loyal to her company for many years, and exciting things were happening currently in her job, which was moving to new technology. She had to wade through some documentation in preparation for tomorrow's meeting where an out-sourcing company was sending representatives to give a briefing and overview on the new technology. She'd asked her fiancé, Mark, not to pop round that evening so that she'd have time to prepare. They were scheduled to get married in 6 months, and the meeting of her natural family was one last action she wanted to complete before saying goodbye to her past life and entering her new life with the person she'd loved for the past 2 years.

Later that evening, after completing all her required reading, she fell into a sound sleep and only woke the next morning to the sound of sparrows in the tree outside her apartment window.

After a caffeine-assisted start, she breezed early into the office and settled into her corner location where she'd spent many happy hours lost in thought working on various programs that were as familiar to her now as the furniture in her apartment.

She stared over the top of her PC as she saw the new consultant on the project walk into the open-plan office. Her jaw dropped as she saw the stunning blue eyes, and observed that under the conservative black suit was a well-toned body. They had been expecting an old and greying ex-mainframe specialist from this long-standing consulting company. This picture didn't seem to fit. Brett was the consultant on the architecture switch from the mainframe to the new object-oriented approach. This was one of the new consultants that Lesley and her colleagues would be spending many months with, learning the new systems and ensuring that the transition from the old to the new would be unnoticed by the millions of customers of this insurance company. They would be getting to know each other very well.

Meetings were the least favourite part of Lesley's job. They had to be done to ensure everyone was coordinated but Lesley preferred to be behind her computer screen, focused on making the system work seamlessly. Her end-users had no clue about the hours of thought and planning put into the programs that ended up on their screens as functioning representations of the financial activities of their lives. By the time they got to see the "front-end" it was friendly, easy to use and made a difference to their lives. Lesley knew this - she didn't need praise for her works of art. It was business as usual for her, but she took great pride in what she did and when she knuckled down to a project, had an incredible ability to focus on the task at hand until it was done.

So this first meeting found her a bit irritable as she'd left a niggly piece of code behind that she hadn't quite resolved yet and still had half her attention on working through that mentally as she sat down at the boardroom with her colleagues and the team of consultants who had flown in from a bigger city to help her company make the transition to the new technology.

She fiddled with the flimsy polystyrene coffee cup that she'd grabbed from the coffee machine en route to the boardroom and made an effort to leave her mental work behind at her comfortable corner location where she preferred to be. This was an important first meeting and she needed to concentrate if she was going to be of any use in the new project.

Introductions were followed by the consulting team's leader giving a very short briefing on the overview of the design to move the company's existing systems across onto the new front-end platform. He outlined the time-line of the project and made it clear that there was a lot of pressure on getting the new system in on time and within budget. There would be overtime and tight deadlines and it was important that the teams work well together and keep their morale up under these pressures.

Then Brett stood up and introduced himself as the chief architect. He outlined the overall design that would accommodate the old system transferring across to the new. As he talked, Lesley started to relax. This guy really knew his stuff and he also fully understood the old mainframe systems her company colleagues were all used to working on. She saw that he was a key player to ensuring that everyone understood the old and the new. She was delighted to realize that the hard work she'd put into preparing for the meeting paid off. The documentation she'd worked so diligently at studying the night before was now making a whole lot more sense as she listened to Brett explain the task at hand.

What a relief! While Lesley was very successful at her work, she always had to work hard at it and the new technology scared her although she wouldn't dare admit that to anyone.

With the closing of the meeting, the various parties went off on their separate ways and got to work on the individual tasks required.

And so, the project rolled out - meetings, coffees, working on code, more meetings. The teams got on pretty well considering they were from very different backgrounds and were specialists in different areas. In fact, Lesley was finding herself really enjoying the times that Brett would need to come and oversee sections of her work. She found him to be a very decent bloke. He seemed to fully grasp how to allay her fears of the unknown and new technology. She grew more and more confident that the project was going to succeed. While sad to see some of her favourite old workhorse programs heading for extinction like plodding old dinosaurs, too big and cumbersome for the world of instant access to the financial world on everyone's home PC, laptop or phone, she was getting more and more excited at how the changing world was actually reflecting in the work she was doing.

Without Brett and his brilliant mind this project could possibly have been headed for disaster. His brilliance extended beyond technical expertise as he seemed to fully grasp the emotional impact on Lesley's team, who were set in their ways and had found a comfort zone in their tried and trusted methods that worked for them but were not going to keep pace with a changing world. He was able to address these softer aspects to the project without making anyone feel foolish or insecure.

As was usual with intense projects, Lesley's personal life suffered to some degree. She saw less and less of Mark over this period. Mark was used to this, but it still put strain on the relationship - particularly as they were now engaged and needed to have the time to start planning their future. They made a point of setting at least one date night per week to catch up and plan.

It was thus with relief that she left the office - late as usual - after the third intense week of pressurized deadlines and made her way to their favourite Italian restaurant to enjoy an evening with Mark and relax a bit.

She walked in to see Mark waiting patiently at their usual table. His eyes lit up as he saw her arriving and he stood to hug her affectionately before they settled to a relaxed meal of laughter, future plans and simply enjoying each other's company after the strain of the past week.

Mark was an architect with his own business. While Lesley was designing bits and bytes, Mark designed beautiful homes. Both were passionate about their careers and so understood each other's needs in their respective professions. Sometimes Lesley couldn't believe her luck that she'd landed such a decent, caring bloke. She'd not had that many boyfriends preceding meeting up with Mark. Unlike her computer programming career, she didn't feel that she excelled in the relationship department and she was just happy that she'd found someone so gentle and kind who wanted to spend the rest of his life with her.

They had a lovely, relaxed evening which passed by all too quickly. Then it was off to bed and an early start for Lesley, who needed to be in early at the office over the weekend to work on some testing on the new project.

The next day she arrived fresh and eager to get going. It was a skeleton team at work and they got down to business straight away as none of them particularly wanted to spend the whole of their weekend in the office.

Brett was there to supervise the parallel testing of the new and old systems and Lesley, being the expert on the old programs she'd worked on for years, was needed to ensure that the new did all the same functionality as the old. There were a few other people from the two teams working happily together, excited to see the new system starting to take shape.

Lesley was deeply engrossed in checking that a particularly complicated function was not compromised in any way on the new system when suddenly she felt a warm hand touching her shoulder as she stared at the screen. "We're getting there!" said the equally warm voice that went with the hand - it was Brett, sharing the moment of triumph as they saw how the efforts of the teams of the past few weeks were finally paying off.

Lesley should have been happy and triumphant - but something churned in her stomach. Something didn't feel right about how Brett had put his hand on her shoulder. It was just a friendly touch - but her instincts told her something was not right. She battled to keep her composure and agreed - "Yes - we're almost there." But she didn't dare look up at Brett - she didn't need to see those stunning blue eyes right now, at such close quarters.

Instead, she started typing furiously on her keyboard to start up the next test and muttered something about getting done so that they could all have a bit of what was left of the weekend. But as she started typing, her fingers shook so much over the keyboard that this didn't help much either. Brett seemed to sense her embarrassment - of course he would be so good at being sensitive to emotions. Damn! Why was he just so perfect in understanding people, so clever, so ... what was Lesley thinking? She took a deep breath as he finally, thankfully, moved off to the next desk to check on her colleague, Susan's work. She looked from the corner of her eye to see that he most definitely did not do anything near to putting his hand on Susan's shoulder. Susan was single, beautiful and available. So what was it with this gesture towards her?

Lesley managed to get through the rest of the work for that day and got out of the office with her mind in a total turmoil. She didn't know what to read in Brett's friendly demeanour. Perhaps he was just being friendly and showing affection after all the long hours of working together. But she knew it wasn't just that. She didn't know what to do. She was confused by all the emotions stirring up in her. Mark was the love of her life. She was so happy he wanted to marry her. They were engaged to be married next spring. But something was happening to her now that she simply didn't understand. She was not looking for someone else. She was happy. But Brett had been in her thoughts in a different way than just as a business consultant since that first day she'd stared over her computer screen at him. She had tried her best to bury any emotions she had felt by focusing on the task at hand. Successfully masking and denying what had been happening, she'd managed to get by. However, this simple little gesture of his today had left her an emotional wreck. To have something coming from Brett towards her made it very, very scary and she just didn't know what to do about how she felt.

Worst of all, she couldn't say a word about this to the person she trusted most in the world who always helped her sort out the more emotional issues of life. She simply couldn't tell Mark about this.

Lesley had been raised by her adoptive mother with old-fashioned values. You don't betray your friends, you keep your word, people should know they can trust you and rely on you. This is how Lesley approached her life. She wasn't interested in messing people around and hurting people.

But now, she was panicking. What was this emotion she felt for Brett? Her world was in turmoil. This is not what she needed so shortly after getting engaged to Mark. This was also not what Mark needed. In fact, she was so confused that she didn't even know what "this" was. She was so unable to confront what had happened that she couldn't put her finger on it. All he'd done was put his hand on her shoulder. He'd not committed any offense. Was this all coming from her imagination? She was so confused she didn't know how she was going to face Mark or get through the rest of the project.

So, she resorted to what she knew always worked to calm herself down in moments of trauma. She went for a long, long walk. She just walked and walked and walked - looking around at the trees and the houses and trying not to think of anything. Eventually she regained enough composure to go home and face Mark, who had been waiting for her to finish at work.

They ordered in pizzas and chatted about this and that. Mark looked at her concernedly and asked if she was feeling alright - saying she looked tired and stressed out. She explained that the project had just got really intense and she was feeling the strain of it. At least the major part would be over in a week's time. The consulting team would be going home and her team would be wrapping up the loose ends and the consulting would be at a long distance from the end of the following week. As she explained this to Mark, she felt a sudden sadness at the prospect of not seeing Brett on a daily basis after the end of the next week.

She was ashamed of herself. Here was this gentle, caring future husband of hers expressing concern over her well-being, and hidden away in her thoughts she was thinking of how she would miss another man! And yet she still couldn't fully understand what exactly she was feeling for Brett.

Making an excuse that she was totally exhausted, she told Mark that she really needed to get to bed and made her way upstairs to the refuge of the bed that she now felt ashamed to be sharing with Mark. She lay there not sleeping at all, even when Mark came to join her - although she pretended that she was fast asleep. Lesley's world was falling apart and she just didn't know what to do.

She decided to focus on something totally different which she hoped would help her through this. It was a week to go before her appointed meeting with her real mother. The project at work was in its final stages, she didn't need to focus so critically on that anymore - the testing was already in place - so now she would focus on this big day and how to face meeting her mother for the first time since she was an hour or so old! Thankful that she'd found something to put her attention on other than her huge turmoil of emotions around a simple affectionate gesture of a business consultant, she finally managed to go to sleep and dreamed of meeting her mother, Nancy.

The next week went by quite quickly. Lesley found every excuse to avoid Brett wherever possible and busied herself with the testing and tweaking of the new system. She was just focusing on her meeting with her real mother. This was a point she'd been waiting for, for so long, and finally it was about to happen.

On the last Thursday there was a final party for the teams involved in the project as a farewell to the consultants who would be flying back late on Friday. Lesley again avoided Brett and managed to get through the party, concentrating on the fact that Friday morning was the appointed time to meet her mother. She'd put in half a day's leave long before so that she could make this crucial appointment. It also gave her an excuse to leave the party before it got too late, and she simply slipped out so that she didn't have to say any goodbyes. She was hoping that once Brett was out of sight he'd very soon be out of mind and she could settle back to her old life which was not so complicated!

The next day she was up bright and early. She dressed in something not too smart, not too casual - wanting to make an effort for her mother, but seeking to appear friendly and relaxed - and made her way to the café where she was to meet her mother Nancy, and her brother. She sat down at the table and ordered a pot of tea. She was too nervous to watch who came in so she faced her back to the entrance into the café and just poured her tea and waited. Before too long, she heard someone approaching behind her and saw the adoption agency lady come around to the front of the table.

Lesley was excited but terribly nervous. The moment had come. Just as she was about to stand to greet her, she felt a warm hand on her shoulder. The adoption lady spoke quietly. "Lesley, here is your mother, Nancy and here is your brother, Breton". As she turned, she saw a greying, kind, older woman's face, her eyes welling up with tears, looking lovingly at her and reaching to embrace her. Then she suddenly saw her brother next to her, having taken his hand off her shoulder and moved round the table to face her. He looked at her with stunning blue eyes filled with love. "Hello sister," said Brett.

The End

# Winds of Life

The wind played softly with the lace curtains draping prettily across the wide window. Gentle flutters of lace brushed lightly over the shiny, oak floor boards. Geraldine sat quietly contemplating the motion and life of this contented wind. More than a breeze, but not too forceful, this wind seemed satisfied with its role in life. She liked that. It brought some calm and peace to her inner thoughts.

Geraldine was disturbed. Life had not been kind to her this past year. Her sister, Kate, whom she adored, had been extremely ill and passed away and the effect of her untimely death had been completely devastating. Not only was the pain of loss unbearable, Geraldine had spent a lot of time away from home, visiting Kate and handling all the arrangements around the unfortunate circumstances.

In turn, this stress had put an immense strain on her marriage of 15 years. No matter how much Geraldine tried to snap out of her sorrow and be the cheerful person she had always been for her husband and children, she was unable to come fully to terms yet with the huge void in her life. John, the love of her life and dear husband, had tried his best and done everything he knew how, to console her. But even he had reached a point where he didn't know what more he could do for her, short of resorting to chemicals to lift her mood; which both of them were adamant was not the long-term solution. They didn't want to set up a habit that they might regret later. Geraldine needed to go through the grieving process and move on. But it was taking time and taking its toll. As a result, the marriage had reached a point of being almost beyond repair.

John and Geraldine had always been the "perfect" couple that others envied. They had the perfect house, the perfect 2 kids - boy and girl - and while John held down the 'perfect' job bringing in an abundance of wealth, Geraldine had the luxury of raising her children and being the 'perfect' wife and companion to John. It seemed that they were living the dream that others only ever did dream about.

It was true - Geraldine loved John with a passion and it had always been so. Her life was what she had envisaged as a young girl when she contemplated getting married and settling down. Everything had gone according to plan.

But this past year, the plan shattered and crumbled and some weak spots in the foundations of this marriage were glaring with ugliness into this idyllic home.

The worst part of it all was that because Geraldine had always had it so easy, she didn't even have any sort of support structure or network to draw on in this time of stress. Because all her friends were envious of her perfect set-up, she felt that she had to uphold the image and didn't dare make any of her marriage problems known, even to her most intimate friends or family members. She was in a fix!

At this stage of the morning, it was all she could do to sit in her chair in the lounge and watch the expensive lace curtains rippling quietly in time to the soft wind. She was alone in the house as her children were staying with John's parents for a week. They had offered to lighten her load by looking after the children for a while during this difficult time.

She had everything she wanted in the world which was of material value - the most gorgeous house, best schools for her children, dinner parties that were a total success, holidays to exotic places. But this didn't fill the hollow emptiness that she was feeling now. She realized that the one thing that money could not buy, her happiness in her marriage and with her family, was under severe and imminent threat. The apparency had always been that money could buy these things, but the sad reality now, was different.

John sat in the business meeting trying his level best to focus on the crucial deal that was being discussed. A lot was depending on the company pulling off this deal. Many things were at stake in terms of his own career path, his image in the company and his future financial well-being. Due to his early successes, he had developed an expensive life-style. He had a huge house and ongoing large expenses to maintain his wife and children in the life-style to which they had grown accustomed. This put ongoing pressure on his performance in this "dog-eat-dog", high-pressured work environment.

And today, those pressures were even greater as he was well aware that his marriage was under the greatest strain it had ever been under in all the years since their perfect wedding on the beach 15 years ago. Men are sometimes considered to be lacking in the softer skills and appear to be less emotional and less aware of these things. John did not suffer from these lacks and although he did not visibly show his emotions to the extent that his sweetheart, Geraldine did, he was churning inside and eaten up with worry about their way forward from where they had landed at this juncture in their lives.

A strong, blustery wind had come up outside the boardroom window. It seemed to symbolize the wild and frenzied emotions he was grappling with. As he gazed numbly at the tall palm tree outside having its fronds torn by the gusts of angry wind, he vaguely became aware of his boss saying his name. "I think John will agree with that, don't you think, John?" he said rather forcefully. John, startled out of his meanderings in his mind, jerked back to the present situation of the crucial meeting. He realized that his boss had done him a favour by drawing his attention back into the boardroom so that he could contribute meaningfully to the discussion at hand. No time for worrying right now about domestic circumstances - that would only compound his problems. He forced his attention back onto the important deal being negotiated.

Geraldine, after moping at the lounge window for some moments, decided she needed to do something positive to get herself lifted out of this state of mind. After all, for 15 years, she and John had managed to work through things and sort out their problems together. For some reason, because her sister was as close to her as John, but in a different way, this sudden loss had unexpectedly impacted every part of their lives. Everything she and John had taken for granted was shaken up. Her view of the things that were important - such as her house, her wealth, her children's good schooling - shattered into insignificance when confronted with the importance of life and love and treasured memories of laughter and happiness. Her world had fallen apart and she'd lost her stability.

Glancing up again at the lace curtains, she saw beyond them that the tree just outside the window was also bending in the wind, which had gathered some strength. This was the tree that she, John and her daughter had planted so lovingly as part of her daughter's school project 7 years ago.

As it leaned over under the pressure of the air rushing through its leaves, one of the green leaves that had been loose ripped off and got carried away on a current of air. Geraldine felt like the leaf. Buffeted about by the winds of life, she no longer felt stable and secure. She was like a loose leaf being pounded around by life's hardships and her frantic emotions. She wished she could be like the green tree - stable within the buffeting of life's winds. If only she could put down her roots deep into the earth and feel as if no amount of wind or disturbance to her happy little family could rip her out. But she didn't feel this was possible right now. Emotionally, she was blowing around, out of control. Something had to be done.

Things couldn't continue in this way. She firmly resolved to do something about it as soon as possible, and not let it wait one more day.

The meeting finally ended and released John to his own private office. He walked from the boardroom to his office in a slight daze. He was usually on top of his game and running ahead of the pack. This was a strange sensation to feel so knocked apart by emotions. He knew he had to get his focus back or things would just get worse. Geraldine was so different and unapproachable at the moment. She had always been his rock, his stable point. He did know and appreciate that a lot of his business success was due to her being there for him through the stresses and strains of his hectically paced career. He would often come home at night and, after the kids were in bed, he'd chat to her about the various deals that were pending. She was an excellent listener and some of his brightest breakthroughs had occurred during these quiet times they had together.

Now, she was immersed in her own troubles and the roles had been reversed. He did not consider himself a good listener. It just didn't come naturally or easily to him. He was used to being the driving force, doing the talking and having others listen to him. He was not handling this period of his marriage very well and he knew it.

Both Geraldine and John loved each other to bits. They had fallen for each other instantaneously when they met through friends 16 years ago. There was never any glimmer of doubt about the fact that they would marry and create their lives together. All had gone smoothly and sometimes to the envy of their peers. And now neither of them possessed the skills to navigate these drastic changes that life's winds had blown their way.

John started to work furiously on the tasks he had set himself for the day. But his mind was not under his usual control. He kept thinking about his beautiful and sad Geraldine and his beloved children. Outside of work, they were John's world. They meant everything to him. He was successful and proud at his work because they supported him and were at his side. There was no joy in his work if he couldn't have his family happy.

John decided as he was usually the one in command, that he would take the initiative, despite the fact that he felt hopelessly incapable in such softer issues of the heart. He was resolved to at least try. His wife and family meant everything to him. He couldn't even contemplate the thought for one second, of losing Geraldine. He suddenly realized in this moment that he would even rather give up his career success than lose her. That was a startling revelation that scared him. He felt as if he was losing control. All his usual actions of success were being threatened in this moment.

It was time to do something effective to prevent a downward slide both personally and in his career that he had worked so hard at for all these years. Now was not the time to let things fall apart.

His mind was made up. There was no point in trying to concentrate further on the project deadline. He couldn't focus anyway. It was time to sort things out one way or another. He picked up the phone.

"Hi Honey," the soft and sad voice of his sweet Geraldine almost whispered at the other end of the line. "I was just about to call you myself when the phone rang. I need to meet with you John, I really need to talk and I'm miserable all on my own here at the house. I can't stand it anymore."

John's heart felt crushed as he heard her voice breaking into sobs. He hated life for doing this to his beautiful wife. It was cruel and he was as mad as the wind outside his office, which seemed hell-bent on ripping the trees outside to shreds.

"Sweetheart, I'm on my way home right now. The office can wait. Just get yourself a cup of tea and relax - I'm heading home."

He sped down the highway, feeling the gusts of wind playing with the motion of his car. This was a typical Cape Town South Easter. Geraldine would always make sure she didn't wear a flaring dress or skirt if the weather threatened to do this. He smiled to himself, thinking of her endearing habits and the special moments they had shared. They had 16 years of their own private jokes and chuckles that only they knew were specially theirs to laugh at. He longed to have her happy again and to pick up the life they had had. But she needed him now and he needed to help her to get through this period. She'd always been there for him and now it was his turn to be the stable rock.

Geraldine heard the all too familiar sound of the key rattling in the door. At last, her darling John was home.

The big, burly frame filled the doorway and filled her with relief. He put his arms solidly around her and held her tight. For that moment, Geraldine felt safe and secure and no longer lonely and in grief. She momentarily forgot her sadness and simply let him hold her. Neither spoke a word. They could both feel the pain slide away for this brief moment as they embraced in their loving world.

Finally, he gently led her to the couch where they sat quietly, looking out of the window. The wind was practically a gale by now. Dandelions were whirling around and her daughter's tree was almost bent in half - then springing back as the gusts abated, only to be pounded once more with the next unseen force.

"See that wind John?" she said softly. "That's life. Life blows these winds at us and we have to go with its flow. I never expected to lose Kate at such a young age. It was so unpredicted. Just like the next gust of wind. That tree doesn't know which way it's going to blow, or which little green leaf it's going to lose next. But it keeps standing strongly in the ground no matter how much it gets blown about."

"Geraldine, Love, you are strong like that tree. You've always been my strong rock that I could depend on and without you I'd never have become what I am today. You've been blown about a lot and I am here for you now. You can depend on me, I promise. I'll see you through this."

He reached out to take her hand as they sat staring through the window which was framed with the lace curtains that were now wildly shuddering in an eerie dance.

"Life also blows good winds, you know," he said gently, squeezing her hand. "Our two lovely kids got blown our way. I'm glad they turned up!"

Geraldine smiled and gave a little light chuckle of relief. "You're right, John. I know I need to look at our blessings, cherish my memories of Kate and move on. She would want us to be happy. She wouldn't want me to be wallowing in grief. She would want me to focus on our future - you, me and the kids. I'll do my best to perk up."

"You know, G, let's turn this around and celebrate Kate's freedom. She's free to make her own way amongst the winds out there and land where she wants to land. She's free to create her life just as we are. Let's celebrate her new life and let her be free to choose which way she wants to blow with the wind today."

"John, you're right. I can let go now. She is free. She's a free spirit - and she always was anyway!"

They held hands more tightly and sat silently watching as the wind blew a loose dandelion through the small gap in the slightly open window. It danced on the current for a few seconds, in mid-air and then landed gently on the frame of Geraldine's favourite photograph of her sister.

Geraldine and John looked at each other and smiled.

"Well, she always was a free spirit and always will be," said Geraldine, getting up to gently take the dandelion off the frame. She stood at the window and blew it back into the wind, where it caught a strong current and was lofted up high and away into the pale sky. They watched it dancing away until they couldn't see it anymore.

"Now, let's plan our day tomorrow. I've taken the day off work and you and I are going to create a fresh day and do with it whatever we want to. The day hasn't been born yet, so let's decide how we will create it for us," said John.

The End

# Romance under the Clouds

(This short story contains some sensitive content.)

A cool breeze played with the long grass as Sarah lay back, looking up at the endless blue of the sky. She had laid out her blanket on the long grass to make a comfortable spot for herself. Whenever Sarah needed to think quietly, she loved to come out here to this fairly wild field behind her house. The yellow daisies waved their sweet heads around in the breeze and cheered her up. She adjusted her head on the sweater that she'd rolled up for use as a pillow, settled into her spot and gazed peacefully into the sky with no end.

Here and there, a little white cloud appeared to break the endless blue. They were travelling along across this vast expanse of space. Sarah liked to find shapes in the clouds. A little one came along that looked like a teapot - she made out the spout and handle. No sooner had she seen the teapot when it dispersed into two separate puffs and they were on their way out of her line of vision.

The reason Sarah had come to her peaceful spot, was that she needed some quiet time and space to think about things. There was too much noise in her head. This was her thinking spot, where no-one would disturb her while she sorted out the whirl of thoughts and questions in her head.

Suddenly, just as Sarah started to really relax and settle down, she heard the sound of someone running very fast towards her. She sat up, startled and frightened - on full alert. Nobody knew she was out here!

"Sarah! I've been looking everywhere for you. We have to talk!" The voice was agitated, but at the same time, the tone was caring.

"Michael! You know this is my private space. This is my sacred spot! Please don't intrude. We're having coffee tomorrow remember? You didn't need to do this!" Sarah's sudden sense of fear turned very quickly to anger.

"Sarah, sweetness, please! I really need to talk. I can't wait until tomorrow. Please, just give me 10 minutes. Then I'll leave you to your thoughts here in your peaceful space." Michael was more earnest than she had ever seen him in the 3 years that they had been together. Now she was caught between her emotions of anger and her deep, deep love that she had felt for this man since the first time she'd met him.

Sarah got annoyed with herself at this point that she just couldn't hold onto her rage. She'd come up here to be alone and really feel this rage. She wanted to feel this intense anger, because she was furious with Michael, and she felt that she needed to stay angry in order to make her next decision. It was pointless making a decision when everything was going sweetly. What about the rough times such as this? Her choices needed to embrace these moments too, as she was the one that would need to live with them if she and Michael were really going to work it out together.

They'd been together for 3 years now and this is how it was. Perfect for a while and all went smoothly. Then, whenever

Michael went out boozing with his friends, a different person came back to the house. Sarah loved and adored the alcohol-free Michael. The other side to Michael, however, was a person that she was not sure she could spend the rest of her life with. And that was why she needed quiet time to think this all through. There was no point in asking someone else's opinion. This was her life, and her choice to make. She would need to face the consequences of her choice, either way.

"Michael, please, you've been drinking and you know that we've agreed not to try and resolve things at times like this. We can talk tomorrow first thing. I'll meet with you at Gina's Coffee Shop. Usual table," said Sarah, appealing to Michael to leave this conversation for another day.

"Sarah, Love, just give me 5 minutes. I can't wait until tomorrow." Michael sat down next to Sarah and held her arm quite forcefully.

Sarah froze. This was her boyfriend of 3 years, but she knew how he could get when he'd had one too many. And here they were, alone on the grass at the back of her

109

house. No-one on earth knew they were there. She knew with all her heart that she loved Michael. But equally, she was aware that the Michael-plus-alcohol combination she'd come to know was another ball-game altogether. He became a different person - not the man she loved. He became threatening and belligerent and had gotten physically threatening on more than one occasion. Her blood turned cold as she felt his grip tighten on her arm.

How could it be that she so loved this man, yet so feared him? She knew the answer. This was not the man she adored; this was a combination of him and alcohol. The two simply did not mix well.

"Michael, please!" she said, trying not to be too pleading and weak, and also trying not to sound too angry, as that would set off *his* anger. She knew she had to play this right as she was all alone out in the back field and didn't even have her 'phone on her. She'd come out here for some peaceful time to think! Not for this.

Even as she lay there with Michael firmly gripping her forearm, she looked past his taught, troubled face and saw her comforting clouds in the blue beyond. She tried to take some strength from their serenity, up there in the sky. She took comfort in the fact that they were there and they would continue to be there, sailing across the blue - no matter what happened next.

All of this seemed to take an age, but probably happened in a few seconds. Michael gripped more tightly, squeezing her arm 'till it throbbed with the stopped blood-flow. He then made a move that sent a surge of raw terror through her entire body. His other hand came towards her neck, while his blood-red face came within inches of hers. The fumes of whisky assailed her senses and she felt herself starting to black out as his hand pushed on the top of her throat.

She battled to focus on the puffy clouds she could still vaguely make out beyond the heavy face of Michael up close against hers. She tried to scream but her airway was blocked. The clouds started blurring and she lost focus and was barely capable of looking the few inches in front of her at Michael's dark eyes. She couldn't utter a sound. In desperation she looked him straight in the eyes and communicated with him silently that way. She saw the anger in his face and suddenly, at this moment, she couldn't feel fear or anger. Looking up and seeing his complete loss of control and his despair, her heart filled with sadness for this man that she so loved, but couldn't live with anymore. As she felt this surge of emotion, she felt the grip loosen and saw a change in his eyes. He seemed to momentarily come to his senses and become aware of what he was doing.

She didn't dare move at this point. Trying not to set him off again, she firstly concentrated on getting some air into her lungs as the airway opened up again under his more relaxed hand. She didn't say anything now. She continued to look up into his deep, dark eyes, which looked almost black to her at this moment. She saw them fill with huge, wet tears.

"Sarah, what am I doing?" he said, suddenly aware of what he was actually doing. "Oh my God, what am I doing?" He took his hand off her throat and pulled away. She lay still, terrified to say anything or do anything that might trigger more violence. She had never seen him so disturbed.

He sat on the grass and held his face in his broad hands, and sobbed and sobbed.

She lay there silently focussing on her clouds up above, watching them gather, then dissipate, then gather, then gently move along. She wished she could just float up there and be with them. Somehow, she needed to get out of this situation. She dare not move and upset him further and decided to let him get rid of all this emotion that had built up inside him. She could feel his anger melting away as the grief poured out. All this emotion seemed to be pouring out as clouds pour out their contents in a rain shower. She allowed him to have his time there in her usually tranquil and special place. Something seemed to be changing.

Finally, the sobs subsided and he turned to her. "Sarah, I know now why you can't stay with me. I see that I'm not the right man for you. I'm sorry. I'll always love you, and I'm sorry I messed up my chances with one of the most beautiful girls, inside and out, that I've ever known. But the right thing to do is to let you be free to move on with your life."

Sarah kept on staring up at the sky and the clouds. This was breaking her heart. She had never, ever seen Michael so distraught and so remorseful. She knew that what he was saying was the truth… *if* he continued to drink. She knew that this was all due to the alcoholic chemicals going into his system and changing him from the sweet man that he actually was, into this monster she'd just experienced. So yes – it was true that he'd messed up his chances and it was true that he should let her move on with his life. But these things were only true about him *plus* the alcohol. They were not true about *him*. He was a good man, and she loved him with all her heart.

"Michael, you need to look after yourself. What you say is right. It breaks my heart to agree with you, but you are right. I need to live my life. I don't want to live it without you, but I also can't live it with you and the drink. We both know it can't work."

Now the tears were flowing freely down *her* cheeks. She had finally said it. She no longer needed to lie there and stare at the clouds or feel that rage. There was no going back now. There was nothing more to think through. The truth was the truth and it hurt.

Michael put his arms around her and held her. He was still far from sober, but his anger had dissipated like the clouds dispersing above in the blue, blue sky with no end. She allowed him to hold her, but it broke her heart more to feel his warmth and care just as they were saying "goodbye".

Feeling completely shattered, she finally looked up at him with her tear-stained face and said softly, "Michael, you need to go now. Please find someone who can help you. I tried and I couldn't, and we need to move on. We both know that you must go now. Otherwise we'll never be able to do it. This is the time to do it. We've held each other and we know we love each other. Let's end it on this note, please, Michael."

Michael listened and nodded. He gave her one more hug and stood up to go. She couldn't look at him. She waited until he had walked some distance and then raised her eyes to see his last steps as he walked around the house to the front where he had parked his truck.

Taking a deep breath, she lay back again and stared at the clouds as she heard him start his engine. She braced herself for the sound of the man she loved, driving away from her house for the last time. This was unbearable. She heard him revving and revving the engine. He was clearly still not in his right mind. But the engine sounded as rough as he looked. Something was wrong with his truck as well as his mind. Suddenly there was a roar of sound as the truck took off, and the next sound was one that would live in her own mind for the rest of her days. There was an almighty crash and splintering of glass, which seared through her senses.

At first, she couldn't move. Her wits froze as she took in what had just occurred. She should never, ever, ever have let him drive in the state he was in. Sarah had been so wrapped up in her own emotions that she hadn't thought this through. Filled with horror at what was awaiting her, she finally found the strength to stand up and she ran as fast as she could towards the place where he always parked his truck, just at the top of the hill.

Blindly running, wiping fresh tears that were streaming down her face, Sarah felt the air burning her lungs as she gasped with the effort of pumping her arms and legs as fast as she possibly could towards the house.

"Sarah! Sarah! Stop!" She felt a vice grip around her arm stopping her but she struggled to keep going, she needed to get to the front to see what had happened to Michael and his truck. Then she realized with a cold terror that there was no-one else around but Michael... So who was shouting at her?

"Sarah! It's Michael! I'm OK. I wasn't in the truck!"

She stopped dead as his grip tightened on her arm and he grabbed both her shoulders and turned her face to look at him. Here was her man, her love, her soul-mate, standing in front of her and looking straight into her eyes. He was alive. He was there, in front of her.

This had been a day from hell. Sarah collapsed, sobbing, into his arms. He held her tightly and stroked her soft, shiny hair, soothing her as she held him and cried until she was done.

"Sarah, sweetheart, I can't leave you now. I have no truck to leave in. I'm so, so, sorry that I messed up time and time again. There was a weird sound in the engine and I got out to check it, forgetting that I'd left the handbrake off. You know I always park just at the top of the hill. Well, gravity got the better of my truck!" he said, waving his arm in the direction of his wrecked truck which had landed up against a massive tree.

"Michael, what are you and I going to do?" asked Sarah at last. She could see that the crash had snapped Michael out of his inebriated state and he was once again the Michael that she wanted to spend the rest of her life with. This was Michael without the poison of the alcohol affecting his mind, his body and his emotions. This was the pure Michael whom she adored with all her heart. He had taken control now and he was now the calm one.

"Michael, when you came up to the back, I'd gone there to think and sort out my thoughts. I did sort them out. I know that I love you, but I love *you*. I don't love you plus alcohol. That's what we have to sort out. It's up to you, Michael." she said gently.

"Sarah, let's go to your spot and talk. You've had your time to think and watch the clouds. I want to do that with you. This affects both of us. I can't leave you to do all the thinking. The least I can do is hear you out and work out a way forward for us. I can't live without you. We have to work this out and I need your help."

They walked, hand-in-hand, to her spot behind the house and lay back on the blanket that was still spread out on the grass. They both gazed up at the clouds in the big, blue sky.

"See those clouds up there, Michael?" she said, pointing to some fluffy little ones that were sailing past. They come and they go. Now - do you see those two joining up there? Look! They are becoming one cloud. That's how it should be with you and me."

"I know, Sarah, I know I need to stop the drinking. We have everything any two people could ever want from each other when I don't put that stuff into my system. You know that I've tried to quit before and it didn't work out. I didn't have enough drive and need to really do it. You have to believe me that that moment has come today for me. The necessity is there. I knew it the moment I saw that truck crash into that big tree. Sorry about your gorgeous tree. That truck is the old me, Sarah, it's finished. My drinking is finished. I've stopped. I'm never, ever, ever going to touch alcohol again as long as I live. I know that that's the only way for me to do it. If I don't, I lose you and if I lose you, I've lost my world."

Sarah took this in. She knew that Michael was telling the truth this time. This time was different from the others. They both looked up at the clouds and saw one cloud start to disperse and disappear, leaving pure, endless blue sky in its place.

"That is what's happened to my need for the drink, Sarah; it's gone - like that cloud. We don't need that clouding our relationship. We need to keep it pure and without poison affecting it. Alcohol is a poison in my body. I've learned a hard lesson. I don't care how much pressure anyone else puts me under to booze it up. I don't care what anyone is celebrating. It's gone from my life. It's gone from our lives."

Sarah listened quietly. She knew Michael. She knew this was not just talk. This was different now. She knew she didn't need to ask how she could trust his word. She knew that this time, he really understood - and he spoke the truth.

"Michael, this is our life. We'll help each other through it. We each have our weaknesses. We each have our strengths. Together, you and I are strong because we have each other's help through the rough times. Without the alcohol we can do it. We can travel through life together and see each other through what will meet us on life's path. But we'll be together in whatever we need to face. I told you I don't want to live my life without you. Now I have you, just you. And that's all I ever wanted."

"Sarah, see those clouds up there? I felt blown around in the winds, just like the clouds. Now see those two clouds joining together? That's us, Sarah. With you at my side, I feel strong and able to create a happy life into the future. No more being blown around. We need to steer our joint course now, backing each other up as we travel through life. Thank you for showing me the truth."

They held each other lovingly and gazed up at the little fluffy clouds breaking up the blue, and then moving along their way. Happiness filled the space and they both felt the sensation simultaneously - a free and floating sensation as if they were joining the clouds up in that endless blue sky.

Michael and Sarah finally knew, with peace, that they could plan their future together.

The End

# Romance in the Sunshine

Genevieve sat contentedly on the old, stone bench out in the soft sunlight. Above her was a magnificent tree. She watched the ground as the rustling wind shifted the leaves playfully above her. As the leaves bobbed around in a little dance to the wind, they played with the shafts of bright sunlight that found their way through the old tree's branches. She watched as the sunlight seemed to daub spots of brightness on the dry earth in front of her. At the same time that the leaves were dancing away, she was also fascinated with the millions of tiny dust specks that waltzed their way into and out of the light shafts thrusting through the leaves.

As she contemplated nature's painting and dancing around her, she felt a warm hand touching her shoulder lightly. There was only one person in the whole world who knew she would be in this spot where she liked to hang out on a lazy Sunday afternoon.

"Hi Ryan," she said happily, without even glancing up.

"It's not Ryan," said a woman's voice.

Within a split second, Genevieve's mood dived from happy and contented to a sudden panic. She knew that voice. It was Holly, a pretty girl who had recently moved into the neighbourhood.

"Holly! How did you know about this spot in the park? Only people who've lived here all their lives know how to find this bench as it's so hidden away in the trees that have grown tall as we grew up here!

"Ryan told me," smiled Holly.

Once again, Genevieve felt cold panic sweep over her. What did Holly have to do with Ryan? Why was Ryan telling Holly about their very special romantic place, where they both loved to come and enjoy the warmth of the sun filtering through the oak tree's leaves?

Genevieve was speechless. She didn't want to show her concern to Holly, not knowing where this conversation was going to go. She pretended that all was fine for Holly to join her on the bench and motioned for her to sit down while she gathered her thoughts. After all, Holly was relatively new in town and Genevieve had gone out of her way to help her to settle in. It was never easy for a newcomer, especially in this town where people had been tight friends for many years. Genevieve's heart went out to Holly when she had arrived on the scene and tried to get to know people around town. Genevieve had even introduced her to Drew, and Holly and Drew had dated briefly although the relationship didn't work out long-term.

So, she allowed Holly to sit next to her. It would only be a matter of minutes before Ryan arrived to join her anyway, then it would be obvious to Holly that they wanted their own time together in this romantic spot.

"I wouldn't wait around for Ryan," said Holly with a slight smirk. "He asked me to pass on a message to you, that he's not stopping by today."

Genevieve felt as if all the blood in her body washed in a wave down to her feet. Her face went pale and she tried to disguise the shock at hearing Holly's words. This was not possible. This couldn't be happening to her. She and Ryan were made for each other. They had been sweethearts for 2 years now and things had been moving in the right direction in their relationship. Or so Genevieve had thought, until this horrible moment.

She sat still, saying nothing as Holly giggled a little nervously next to her. Genevieve focused all her attention on the shadows and sunspots appearing and disappearing on the hard earth beneath the huge oak tree. She was determined not to show any emotions to Holly. That smirk had not been her imagination. Her mind reeled with a myriad of thoughts as she tried to figure out what was happening. Her whole world seemed to be falling apart from that short message that Holly passed on to her.

Was Ryan keen on Holly? Why couldn't he have discussed it with her? Why send Holly to give the message? He'd broken a sacred tradition by not arriving for their Sunday afternoon romantic time on their old bench under the oak tree. More than this, he'd sent Holly to let her know!

Genevieve had way too much pride to discuss this any further with Holly. She didn't look to her side to see Holly. She kept looking down and focusing on the sunlight and shadows on the ground. Without a word, she stood up quietly and walked away, leaving Holly sitting on the bench without further power over her.

As Genevieve increased her distance from Holly and walked briskly out into the glaring sunlight, the tears came flooding down her face. She didn't know what to do, where to go or who to talk to. She was devastated. She hoped with all her heart that Holly wasn't following her and she didn't dare look behind.

Walking as fast as possible, practically blinded by her streaming tears, Genevieve headed for the old stile in the shrubbery where she and Ryan always made their way over the wooden fence, using its rickety wooden steps to assist them to climb over.

All of a sudden, she saw a familiar figure negotiating the stile. So many times, she and Ryan had laughed happily as he helped her over, pretending she was a gracious lady and he was her knight. Then she'd giggle mercilessly as he tumbled over, in a hurry to sweep her off her feet and kiss her as they fell, collapsing in a heap in the long, green grass.

There was no laughter now, as Genevieve recognized Ryan's butt and long legs coming over the stile. She froze on the spot, not knowing where to run or what to do. So instead, she just stood there in the long grass and watched as Ryan started heading in the direction of their sacred spot.

Suddenly, he saw her.

"Gen! I'm coming! Why aren't you under our oak tree?" called Ryan, starting to move faster as he approached her. Seeing her tear-streaked face, his own face tightened with concern.

"What's happened, Baby? What's going on? I wasn't that late. Please, Gen, my sweet Lady, forgive me for being 4 and a half minutes late!" he said, dropping onto his knees and starting to play the knight and the lady.

Now Genevieve was once again in a total turmoil. She just didn't understand what was happening to her beautiful Sunday afternoon in the sunshine. Ryan, seeing that his beloved Gen was in a state, opted not to say anything further or ask anything right at this moment. He stood up, put his arms around her and held her tight as she finished sobbing and calmed down.

"Holly said you weren't coming," she said finally, as he gently stroked her hair away from her face.

"Holly is not my personal assistant! I would never pass a message to you via Holly!" said Ryan, starting to get very heated now that he saw what had happened.

In that moment, Genevieve learned a very valuable lesson. She was ashamed that her trust in Ryan had been shaken. It had been shaken because she believed what someone else said about him, rather than waiting to clarify directly with him. She vowed in that instant, never to ever let that happen again. Holly had smirked and given her a negative message about her beloved Ryan – but Ryan wasn't there to defend himself. Holly meant mischief. Well, she was not going to win this one.

"Ryan, let's go and find Holly and sort this all out. She's in our sacred place. I don't know how she knew I'd be there, or that you'd be meeting me there."

Ryan suddenly looked sheepish. "Well, Gen, it is partly my fault. I will explain, I promise!"

Genevieve couldn't stand for more mystery and confusion. All she wanted to do right now was to sit with Ryan on her romantic old stone bench and get her bearings. This had all been too much for her.

They made their way, arm-in-arm towards their big oak tree and the old stone bench. Genevieve didn't know whether Holly would still be there but she knew that Ryan would handle things. She didn't care now, if Holly saw that she'd been upset, because her man was at her side and holding her, and the threat of losing him was over.

The sun was shining warmly down on the path and as they approached the tree, she saw that Holly wasn't there. It would just be Ryan and her in their Sunday afternoon spot. The only visitor was the warm sun, sending playful beams down through the leaves to kiss the ground and to touch their shoulders and heads as they sat on their special bench.

"Gen, my sweet Lady, this was supposed to be our place in the sun. I'm sorry it went awry. It was just one big mix-up!"

"Ryan, I'm sorry. When Holly said you weren't coming, I panicked. I know I should have trusted you. I just couldn't believe it and I didn't know how Holly knew where you and I would be meeting. Not many people have even found this little spot here because it's so hidden away in our big park. "

"Gen, there's only one reason that Holly knew I'd be joining you and that I'd be late. She must have followed you here. She was in the florist where I went to get you something special for tonight. It was supposed to be a surprise – but I was running so late by the time I got into the shop, and I mentioned that as I was dashing out. So she knew that I'd still need to take the flowers home first before meeting you. I bet she saw you walking past her place on the way to the park and she followed you to our spot.

Suddenly they heard a rustling behind the tree. They both stared as Holly came out from where she'd been hiding all this time.

"Genevieve, Ryan, I am so, so sorry. I don't know what to do to properly apologise to you both. I was really nasty and I want to somehow make it up to you both. I'm sorry, Gen. I'm a jealous person. You are so pretty and you got such a gorgeous guy. I'm just a jealous and bitter person," said Holly, breaking down into tears.

Gen looked at her in disbelief. Now it was Holly's turn to hurt! She had no idea. She'd always thought Holly was such a popular, attractive girl with a perfect body. How on earth could she be jealous of her? Gen was modest and considered herself rather plain looking, but she definitely knew she was lucky having found Ryan.

"Hey Holly! It's OK," said Gen, standing up to give her a hug and calm her down. "There's no need to be jealous. You are a gorgeous-looking girl. But if you interfere with other people's relationships, then that's the way not to find your own boyfriend, Holly. Guys want to meet nice girls, who care for them and others."

"I know, Gen," sobbed Holly. "I've been so bitter and twisted about relationships since Drew called it off. I became nasty towards anyone who had a happy relationship. I'm really sorry. I've learned my lesson."

"Well, Holly," said Ryan suddenly, "Do you know that Tom has his eye on you? He asked me if I could help him get an introduction to you just the other day. I didn't realize that Drew and you were totally finished – otherwise I would have spoken to you sooner. But it's just as well that you learned your lesson first. Tom is not the kind of guy that wants a spiteful girlfriend."

"Let's the three of us just agree to never discuss this again. I think we've all learned out lessons," said Genevieve kindly. "Ryan, why don't you call Tom later and set up a date for the four of us. We can go to that new restaurant that just opened up and try out their food."

Holly calmed down and felt very embarrassed, but started to feel much better. She'd taken a good look at things in these few moments and had realized that the way to go forward was to stay honest and keep out of others' relationships. She had always been a good person, and she realized that it was really silly to let one break-up cloud the rest of her life in terms of relationships. She also realized that she'd tried to hurt two of the best friends she had ever had. Ryan and Genevieve were going out of their way to forgive her and help her. Holly began to realize that she was not a victim at all, but she was actually incredibly lucky to know such good people.

"Gen and Ryan, I'll never, ever forget what you've done for me or taught me today. I want to thank you from the bottom of my heart. I'll live up to what you expect of me. You've given me a second chance to be myself again. I'm going to go now, and leave you in your romantic place so that you can enjoy your special time together. Please let me know about Tom and when we'll be doing dinner. It's on me!"

They hugged quickly and Holly was off – practically leaping over the stile with renewed energy as she felt as light as a feather with the relief of having spilled her emotions and confronted the truth with her friends.

Gen settled down on the bench next to her beloved Ryan with a huge sigh of relief too. "Oh, my goodness! I have learned my lesson the hard way. When someone says something bad about someone, make sure you get the truth and don't take another person's word for it. Always talk to the person and make sure of the facts. Life could have gone horribly wrong if I'd not seen you climbing over that stile and bumped into you!"

"Yes, Gen, we must always talk things through directly with each other. Don't listen to somebody else's opinion. Love is between you and me. It's ours to work out for us."

Genevieve sat quietly enjoying the moment, happy that she had such a sensible man at her side.

"Look at the sun playing tricks with the light!" she said, pointing to the dancing sunbeams in front of them.

They both knew that they were safe with each other, and no-one could play any more tricks on them as they moved into their future together. Their future would be bright and sunny, with clear and honest communication, not tainted with hearsay.

The End

# Romance in the Springtime

Katy headed at a brisk pace in the direction of the pink, gabled gazebo. The gazebo was loaded with memories and emotions for Katy. She was home visiting her parents and whenever she came home, she loved to enjoy the garden where she'd romped around as a child. It was amusing to her to see how small everything looked now in comparison to when she was growing up.

The pink gazebo was pink because Katy had painted it pink one summer! It was here that she had played with her dolls as a toddler, had "tea parties" with her friends as a young girl – with lemonade in the tea cups - and it was here, too, many years later, on that beautifully romantic day, when she and John had first found out there was a spark between them that felt like a lot more than just friendship. Katy would never forget that electric moment between John and herself.

Now they had been dating for over 18 months, and their lives had settled into a routine as if they were already a married couple. Although they had each retained their own apartment for now, they felt so settled in life and comfortable with each other that people saw them as a permanent couple. It made sense then, that they should start their plans for engagement and marriage.

Yet there was a sense of anxiety in Katy. She should be happy that she'd found a man whom she loved, and who was also her best friend. She and John were practically inseparable. All their friends considered them to be a stable couple and knew that it would just be a matter of time before they announced their wedding day.

So why, then, did this fill Katy with apprehension? She had come out to her parent's home to have a bit of a break from work and to sort things out in her mind. John was on a business trip and was out of the country. And Katy knew that she had to resolve this inner turmoil for her own sake and also for John's. She loved John with all her heart, and didn't want to hurt him. The closer they were to making their relationship legally permanent, the more frantic she was becoming. She couldn't let this carry on without speaking to somebody. The worst part was she simply couldn't put her finger on what exactly was bothering her.

Katy got to her special place – her pink gazebo at the bottom of the lush garden. Here she could sit in peace in one of the wicker chairs and get some clarity in her thoughts. She positioned her chair so that she could see the sparkling fountain out on the lawn. Katy had purchased the solar fountain for her parents last year. It was in the shape of a lily leaf floating on a mini pond and it sprayed water high up into the air until it fell back down again with a soothing, tinkling sound. Powered by the bright sun, the invisible solar rays drove this little pump to keep on shooting the water up all through the day – until a cloud passed over, weakening its direct power to such an extent that the water would stop abruptly with each passing cloud, only to start up again relentlessly as the bright sunshine reappeared. During the sunny periods, while the water was spraying up in beautiful, glistening droplets, it was a harmony of nature's power and human invention, bringing pleasure to her peaceful place.

Katy enjoyed the familiar fragrance of the fresh, spring blossoms opening their little heads to embrace those same life-giving sunbeams. A light breeze brought along different perfumes of nature, far more delightful and delicate than most of the expensive perfumes available in the shiny store windows in the shopping mall.

Just as the clouds cast their shadows from time to time over the water pump's solar panel, blocking its source of energy, so Katy felt about her current relationship with John. At times, their love and happiness would surge with a powerful energy, just like the spraying water. Then at other times, their relationship seemed to lack a purpose – it just floated along without any real excitement.

This was the clue to what was troubling Katy. She realized she couldn't commit to marriage if their relationship was going to wander aimlessly along, pleasant but nothing special, content but lacking spark. It was nice to be with John. She really adored him. But she thought about the fairly dull routine and humdrum existence they were starting to lead back in the little suburb where they lived and worked. Something definitely had to change.

Katy enjoyed a few more moments in her tranquil pink gazebo, taking in the fresh, green foliage that was thrusting up out of the ground all around her. She loved the springtime! She loved the new growth and new life. She suddenly had a vivid memory of how she used to enjoy painting. She had done so many paintings and sketches of this very garden. Life had become so hectic that Katy hadn't done any painting or any of her own creating in years. Those were her happiest times, when she was creating her own art from her own world, but interacting with the beauties of the physical world around her. Katy was ready to start creating again, just like the spring day. And Katy was ready for some new plans.

After lunch, Katy called up one of her best friends, Karen.

"Karen, can we meet for coffee at our usual place? I'm home for the weekend and

I'd really like to see you. There's also something I want to chat to you about."

"Sure Katy! It will be lovely to see you!"

The two friends met later on that afternoon at their favourite spot. It was a coffee shop that had been in town ever since they could remember, run by Aunt Joy – who was everyone in town's "aunt". Somehow, when you went to Joy's Coffee Shop and relaxed there for a while, you started to see your problems and the world differently. Joy's was a world away from the world and something about the space gave one a good feeling and helped to give perspective.

Perhaps it was simply the warm, personal touch and old-fashioned care and communication that calmed people down. People would stop in Joy's Coffee shop to take a break from their hectic lives of fast electronic communication to "friends" they had never even met in the flesh, but had befriended via a screen image. Here, in Joy's Coffees, you could go back to human interaction – you could embrace a person and feel their warmth, and see clearly, the expression on their face as you chatted. There was something about this that provided a lot of comfort and warmth in the rat-race world of cyberspace and mobile phone screens that everyone was caught up in.

Today, being spring, the little hanging pot plants were ablaze with colour. They hung outside the coffee shop, brightening up the road and they also hung inside, giving a sensation of new life and joy, in keeping with the coffee shop's namesake.

Katy walked in to see her friend, Karen, already ensconced in their usual comfortable corner seat. Karen jumped up to hug Katy "hello" and the girls sat down to chat and catch up on all their news.

Sipping on her Earl Grey tea, Katy finally moved the conversation into what was eating her up inside and giving her sleepless nights.

"Karen, you're my best friend, and I don't know who else to talk to about this. My mom wouldn't really understand." Her voice quavered a little as she realized how disturbed she had actually become at the current state of her life.

"Shoot, Katy, I'm all ears," said Karen sweetly. She had always been a good listener and she herself had had her fair share of heartbreak, having lost her boyfriend, Doug, 2 years ago due to a tragic accident.

"Karen, you know that John and I have been together for some time now. He's a great guy. We are really comfortable together. But our relationship is lacking something. I sat in my pink gazebo this morning and thought it through. It seems that we don't have joint goals – we aren't going for anything together in our lives. John has his business projects; I have my job and my interests. We do well, we make money and we just sort of float along with no plan. Our relationship has become quite stale. John is a good man. I don't want to hurt him, Karen, but I can't really see a future for us long-term."

As Katy spoke, the quavering in her voice intensified and she broke into soft sobs. She only realized now as she talked about it to a good listener, how much pent-up emotion she had stifled inside her. She felt a little embarrassed that she was making such a meal out of something that would not appear to be a big problem to another, but this was how it was for her right now, and she needed some help. She was lost in her own pain at the thought of harming John and facing life again as a single person. But she also didn't want to get trapped into a monotonous life with a partner who wasn't totally suitable.

Aunt Joy was a sharp old lady and she caught a glimpse of the 2 girls deep in conversation. She wisely left them to it, making sure they did not get disturbed at this crucial moment. Over the years, she had seen it all. That was another thing that made her coffee shop so special. It wasn't a robotically run business where staff were trained to do things without any individual thought. This was a place with old-fashioned manners and communication and heart.

Katy finally wiped away her tears and looked up at Karen. With shock, she saw the tears streaming down Karen's face, and a strange look came over her.

"Katy, my dear friend Katy, don't talk to me about this, please! You shouldn't be talking to me about things so dear to you when there is someone else you should be talking to."

"I'm so sorry, Karen – I didn't mean to upset you. Help me out of this, who should I be talking to?"

"Katy, do you know how many times I've regretted not sharing my deepest feelings with Doug? All the things that I should have said and didn't. Then I spoke to other people about it instead of working things out directly with him. Who knows what might not have happened if I'd been more honest and open with Doug.

How will you ever work out any relationship with a person so close to you, if you talk about him to other people instead of talking with him directly? How will he ever know what you need, what you want in your life, if you don't communicate with him? Must he smell it through the spring blossoms?

Don't leave him in a mystery and then move on to another man, not sorting out what you need to sort out. I lost my chance, Katy. One day I hope to meet another man – but I lost my chance with Doug. I'm sorry to talk harshly to you, but please, don't mess up a chance that you still have with a decent guy. You don't know what you will find out unless you actually talk! And not to me, not to your mom, or anyone else – talk to him and take your chances! It seems that you've reached the point where you have nothing to lose anyway. But, gosh, if he turns out to be the right guy for you, Katy, you have everything to lose if you don't just sit down and talk."

Katy stared at her best friend in shocked silence. She had never heard Karen talk like this before. She also knew that what Karen was saying was true. And she felt terrible that she had stirred up Karen's pain and loss concerning Doug.

"Karen, I am so, so sorry. I was so wrapped up in myself and my own problems and worries that I didn't think before I spoke. I don't know how to make this right. You are such a good, dear friend and I have hurt you today."

"Shh... Katy, said Karen, putting her hand on hers. If I can help you to work things out with a man who is good for you, it can take away some of my pain for not having worked things out with Doug before he left me forever. "

The girls sat quietly, taking comfort in each other's presence. This was a turning point for Katy. She realized that not only did she have a friend in a million in Karen, who had the guts to speak out and not go into agreement with her negativity about her boyfriend, but she also realized that she had been going about this the wrong way. Exactly as Karen had said, Katy needed to set up some special one-on-one time with John and work things out directly with him. She was really lucky that Karen wasn't a girl who just weakly listened to her and made her feel "good" by agreeing with her complaints. Karen was kind enough to be honest and to help her to see what to do.

"You know, I love this place and how Joy makes it look so warm and inviting. Look at those beautiful blossoms in the pots!" said Katy gently, trying to cheer up her friend.

"Yes! It's spring! I love spring. There is so much new life around. It's time for both of us to move on and create our lives newly. It's actually OK that I got upset,

Katy. I have been hanging onto those regrets for too long now, and you've helped me to communicate about it."

The girls smiled happily at each other, each starting to think forward into their future. Joy came over with her cheery face to offer them another drink and brought along some home-baked cookies that she was testing out.

A week later, John was back from his business trip and Katy invited him on a "date". The date was a home-cooked meal that Katy prepared with care in her apartment. She had made the space look really nice, with fresh, spring flowers decorating the space. After dinner, they sat comfortably in her living room.

"John, I would like to talk to you about something quite important,' said Katy, letting John know that she needed his full attention. He switched off his mobile phone and Katy did the same. There was no TV playing. This was going to be a good, old-fashioned, live, heart-to-heart conversation.

And so Katy spilled her heart out to John. She told him about her thoughts in the pink gazebo; she told him how she missed her painting and how she felt they didn't have any joint goals. She also told him how much she loved him, how Karen had set her straight and that she was now laying it all on the line so that he could air his views too and they could work out where to go from here.

"Katy, thank you. You have a really good friend in Karen. I think she has done us both a huge favour. I knew something was not right with us, but I also couldn't put my finger on it. Do you know that I actually hate my business! I never dared to tell you, because I thought you were impressed and I didn't want to burst that bubble. The reason I work so hard at it is because I want to make something of myself and get enough money into my account to make you happy. But I realize now that I never bothered to ask you what actually would make you happy. I never knew that you painted! That's so cool! I used to love my photography. I gave that up years ago when I got into the game of chasing money. I'd like to do that again."

This was the beginning of their own springtime as a couple. They had many more dates after that and worked out their actual goals and plans in life. They found out that they had a lot of very important things in common that had nothing to do with money. But strangely enough, as Katy started painting more and as John got back to his photography, they both started to see how their passions in life could also start bringing in some cash – for doing what they loved.

John introduced his best friend, Don, to Karen and things worked out with them too. It was a glorious springtime for everyone. The world looked fresh and new and they all felt ready to take it on. They were following their own dreams, not dreams dictated to them by what the rest of the society was expecting them to do.

One morning, John, Katy, Don and Karen all met at Joy's coffee shop. Katy thought briefly about the solar water fountain and her pink gazebo. As Joy smiled over at her happy customers, the surge of energy and life in her coffee shop was like the spraying water from the lily leaf. Life was exciting again and full of promise. It was up to them to keep the springtime created in their lives, regardless of the external season.

The End

# Romantic River

Jessica lay back in the tall grass and gazed lazily at the blue, blue sky. She wondered how this sky could go on and on with no end and yet it must end somewhere?

It was a Sunday afternoon and every creature and growing thing seemed to be aware that this was a time to rest, reflect and have some peace. Even the quietly swaying fronds of the huge willow tree dipped their ends more lethargically into the pristine water of the river running close by.

This was the spot Jessica always came to when she wanted her own time. It had been a hectic year with lots of accomplishments and she'd met her targets and made all the business goals she'd set herself. After basking in the initial joys of a job well done, Jessica turned inward to reflect on what still needed to be achieved. The celebrations were over and that was a time now in the past. Short-lived are these gossamer goals that, once achieved, become moments in the past, and only the memories and physical objects of accomplishment remain. But time marches and marches into the future!

So now, in these moments Jessica was enjoying the sensation of slowing down the march of time and enjoying the present. The brightly coloured barbet bird was trilling gently in the willow tree, leaves fluttered listlessly on the lower-lying bushes alongside the river and the sparkling water kept up its pace, flowing relentlessly down towards its ocean destination hundreds of miles away.

Jessica had grown up in a large house, on a large property which bordered on a nature reserve. The property encompassed this section of river and thus, her family "owned" this portion of the river as it was in their land. But did they really own this water that kept arriving and then disappearing? This water seemed to arrive and disappear the same way that love arrived and disappeared in her life.

Jessica loved to come home whenever she had a gap from her whirlwind life of meetings and deadlines and would spend time in this spot by her river. Despite the fact that the river kept running, it seemed to slow time down. Jessica always wondered about that, because whenever *she* was running, time seemed to disappear from her! Perhaps she could learn something from her sparkling river today.

During this past year, Jessica had conquered time so often on her different projects and deadlines. She had produced fantastic results in her sales position at an engineering company and had been accordingly rewarded both financially and with a promotion. Jessica was proud of her achievements, yet she still didn't feel satisfied with her life.

Her career was one area where Jessica could plan, work hard and meet her targets. She had always been good at this and felt completely in command of this part of her life. However, when it came to personal relationships, and the area of love and romance, this was where Jessica was simply not able to be as successful as in the work environment. If only a relationship could be project-managed as simply as a work assignment!

But at university where she'd studied engineering, love and romance was definitely not an optional subject and no-one ever thought to include that in any school curriculum anywhere. Yet surely that was just as important to learn so that one could apply this subject successfully in life as with any other of life's games?

Or was this just supposed to be a matter of luck and fate? Having an engineering background and way of thinking, Jessica couldn't accept this. There must be some rules to the game of love, just as there were rules to building a bridge so that it would never collapse. Nature had rules to follow to ensure that things didn't break, so surely there should be some guidelines to ensure that relationships wouldn't break?

As she lay there in the grass, watching a couple of clouds forming in the blue, blue sky and listening to the steady rush of water hurtling forward, Jessica contemplated these things and decided this year, to make a new set of resolutions. She'd proven she could set and achieve her work goals. Now it was time to turn her methodical and organized mind to matters of the heart. As she lay there, she heard the quiet honk of a beautiful Egyptian goose that had settled across the river on the bank adjoining the nature reserve. Seconds later, with a honking flutter, her mate alighted just next to her. He rubbed her neck lovingly with his, and they both gently caressed each other in their graceful way.

Jessica watched the little scene of love and thought how nature seemed to have this relationship thing really simplified. Perhaps she could learn from these beautiful Egyptian geese. Her Dad had told her many years ago that these geese, who were a type of duck, mated for life. They stayed true to each other without the need for formal wedding vows. And how many times had Jessica seen friends and acquaintances swear these vows to each other in solemn moments, only to end up in the divorce court some years later. So perhaps the geese could teach her more than the formal system of vows and contracts.

Thinking back to her last year, she felt an anxiety about how her last relationship with Mark had ended and how they'd parted ways. Mark had been one of the nicest men she'd ever dated. Her parents had liked him and he seemed to be everything she needed in a man. But somehow, this relationship just didn't work out as well as her sales projects and targets. They both blamed their busy lifestyles and had parted amicably, but *there* was a project that had failed, an opportunity wasted. All the potential was there and yet this almost perfect, meant-to-be relationship had dissolved and disappeared like the rushing water disappearing down the river on its way to the ocean.

Surely Jessica and Mark had missed something here. Everything had seemed perfect. They got on well, they enjoyed activities together, but it didn't last. And it wasn't even that they'd had a huge fight and a dramatic break-up. They just drifted apart and had a civilized discussion about it and went off their separate ways. Neither of them was happy. So, something here was wrong. Jessica was determined to get to the bottom of this and apply her mind to seeing a way forward for herself in this failed area of her life.

She looked up again at the little clouds that had formed and were starting to drift like cotton wool balls across the sky. They too were moving along towards their destination just like the river. Jessica decided that unless she sorted out her life soon, she'd be like a lost little cloud just drifting along, prettying up the sky and then moving on, with no purpose and no plan. This didn't suit her. She was used to being in command and in control of things. Why should that not also apply to matters of love?

But love was unpredictable and love was from the heart. Love is not a work project with time-lines and targets and deliverables. That's what made love, love. So how could she apply her engineering mind to this area of her life and be successful without also running it as a business project, because that, clearly, could never work in matters of the heart. A bridge made of bricks and steel was not life. Jessica could handle and plan a bridge but how does one get in control of matters of the heart? A heart is not made of bricks. Life is a flow and it contains surprises and creations; and in a relationship, it contains another person's ideas and life and creations.

Suddenly, she looked back at the river and realized something. The river kept flowing. It had life! It also had unpredictability - would someone dam it up? Would there be an unexpected drought, lessening the water supply from the mountains? Would someone try and catch fish in this water, or put their canoe in it and change some of its flows?

And yet, despite these variables, the river continued to flow and its waters continued to flow together toward a destination far away. Isn't that similar to love? To a bond of people? They are flowing toward an unknown destination far away. The water that Jessica was watching had no clue about the ocean it was going to. Right now it was simply moving along with the rest of the water - moving through time while time stood still for Jessica.

Obviously, there is a big difference, Jessica thought. Human beings can think and plan and decide on directions in their lives. But something could be learned here. The water had life, the Egyptian geese had life, and the clouds in the sky had life. The source of this life was not part of her analysis - enough to realize that they had life and were in harmony with other life. That's what she wanted to achieve in her next relationship. Harmony with another life. So she was definitely onto something here and she lay back to relax and simply enjoy the moment of now, and to contemplate that she had found something helpful in the beautiful nature around her.

She'd learned this tactic on her work projects. When you have a good moment, take the time to have that moment and acknowledge it. That made the moment belong to you so that it was yours to keep along with other good memories. Store up the good moments and the good memories as these can help you through the rough times! Because when projects are sometimes on the brink of disaster or sales deals don't come through, you have successes to draw on from the past and if you don't store them away positively and with awareness, when the bad things happen they can overwhelm and consume your present and you forget all the good things you've done and achieved.

So, having taken stock of this little moment of realization, Jessica looked for some other clues here that she could apply to make her next relationship successful. As no-one had given her a manual for love she realized she needed to figure it out herself. Then the next bright idea came. As the water continued to thunder gently onwards, it occurred to Jessica that without the firm, solid river banks on each side of this water, the water would just wander off in various directions as gravity took it. It was the river banks that held this water together. These real and solid banks had formed through years and years of water carving into the soil and rocks. So this was something real and solid holding this water together and she could understand this concept, like the understanding she'd studied about building a bridge to defy gravity. This was something that she could possibly work with in sorting out what had gone wrong in her relationships.

That was the missing clue Jessica had needed to solve her personal puzzle of how her relationships had been failing. The relationship needed river banks to hold it steady on its course. The water was alive and moving forward in time, subject to changes and unpredictabilities. But as long as the banks held the water together, it flowed in one direction toward a common destination. This made more engineering sense to her than marriage vows without something to back them up. Now she had something to back up any promises she would make in the future. Jessica felt she understood things now, and felt very happy, calm and at peace in her special spot. She sighed gently and looked again at the spot where the clouds had been - they were gone.

A couple of weeks later, back at her hectic engineering sales manager job, Jessica felt rejuvenated and ready to face the year ahead. She walked around the office with a bounce in her step and was even more efficient than the previous year in handling her pressures and targets. Her colleagues started to suspect that she was in love again and had found a new man. But she hadn't. She had just found her clue and this alone gave her such a sense of peace and stability, that it reflected through all her actions.

One morning, while going through her day's agenda and checking the meetings set up for the day, an email popped up from Mark. Her heart stopped briefly and her new-found stability wobbled slightly. Then Jessica remembered the river banks, took a deep breath, and opened up the email.

"Hi Jess, been thinking about you a lot lately...are you up for a coffee after work?"

Jessica smiled as she thought about Mark and his succinct way of communicating when it came to emails. She realized that he had decided not to call as that might be too much all at once for her to deal with, so soon after they'd broken up. As Jessica felt good within herself, and was not in any new relationship, she decided that there was nothing to lose as they'd agreed it would be OK to remain friends if that was possible for them both. She politely accepted his invitation and they agreed on the coffee shop midway between their two offices.

The coffee shop was in a little section of the city with outdoor cafes arranged around a large, cobble-stoned square. They both loved this area of the city as it gave a respite from the rush and noise of traffic, and it gave them some open air space where one could enjoy a cup of coffee and for that moment in time, one could pretend to be in a little quiet village anywhere on the planet.

She arrived on time to find Mark already seated at their favourite table overlooking the fountains in the square. This was a tranquil place and she felt stirring emotions as she approached the table. Mark really was a handsome man but what had initially attracted her to him was not so much that, but his calm and relaxed manner, which so nicely counterpointed her tendency to be rushed and hectic. She felt a little out of control as she sat down, not knowing what to do with the emotions rushing through her. They had mutually called off the relationship and had agreed to part ways. She'd gone to her quiet place by the river in her holidays to help herself to get over this and move on. She'd made peace with the future plans and was set on moving forward.

Now she was approaching awfully close to this man that she'd loved for two years. They'd laughed together, planned together, created a section of their unique lives together. This was proving to be a lot trickier than she'd thought when she'd so glibly pressed the "send" button on the email, accepting his invitation for a coffee on a friendship basis. Electronic email communication can be so easy and shallow. But here they were, facing each other again as live beings, about to communicate in the old-fashioned, live way, not through bits and bytes and electronics.

She suddenly thought about the beautiful Egyptian geese. They didn't have emails, yet they stayed together for life. They caressed each other and communicated through their movements and touches which they could experience first-hand, not through an impersonal computer screen.

"Hi", she ventured, nervously, as she sat next to him but not too close.

"Hi Jess, I miss you," said Mark - straight to the point as usual.

Jessica's heart tumbled and she blushed from the nape of her neck to the roots of her hair. She had definitely not expected this. She hadn't planned for the coffee date as friends to open with this line from Mark. This had not been on her agenda for this meeting. But then this was not business, this was about love and past love and emotions. She sat for a moment trying to catch her breath and regain her composure. Without giving her a chance, Mark continued.

"Jess, you and I are supposed to be together. I can't do this journey through life without you. I know things didn't work out and I know what we agreed, but I want you in my life's journey. I want to do things with you, share in your pleasures, and also share in your problems. I know I was rough with you and I know that I didn't like your complaints about all your work pressures. I want to try this all again. We can work it out if we work at it."

Jessica looked up at this man whom she knew she really did love. He had so many qualities that she'd longed for in a mate. Memories of how she'd utterly adored him when they'd first started dating came flooding back. But she also didn't want to make the same mistakes again and go through heartbreak. She looked up at his deep, soulful brown eyes and saw that they were brimming with tears. This was a little more than she could stand, out here in the open with people walking by.

She didn't say anything for some time. She needed time to assimilate all of this. She looked away from the tears in his eyes to the water of the fountains and thought again about the rushing water of the river in her special place. This was life. This was one of those unpredictable moments. This was what she needed to learn how to handle so that she could keep her life's course steady.

She needed river banks! They needed a stable structure to nurture their love and keep it flowing along in the same direction, to the same goals.

She looked across at Mark and realized that they could do this. It was going to take a lot of communication and a lot of working out what was right for both of them, but they could do this. They could do this thing called life together. They both needed to stay inside the same river banks and flow together toward the same ocean. She decided to jump in and swim.

"Ok Mark, let's give it another go. I want you to take time off this weekend to come with me to my special place though, so we can talk about it. I want to show you some things."

He reached out towards her and put his strong arms around her and held her so tightly that she again couldn't get her breath. He held her close for a few moments. Then they sat quietly drinking their coffee and looking at the fountains and the blue sky. Two little fluffy clouds were scudding across until the one merged with the other.

Two days later, Mark and Jessica lay in the long grass next to her childhood river. Her parents had been thrilled to hear that they were back together but they knew that Mark and Jessica needed some time on their own.

They lay there on the grass and Jessica shared her intimate thoughts with Mark about how she saw their path forward in life. He listened attentively while she told him about the river and the banks and that they needed to establish some banks to keep them together in their channel forward. They had to agree on what that would be for them. Their banks belonged to their river, no-one else's. They had some work to do. Mark got it. He understood.

"We'll have to have lots of dates to work out our river banks. Then we'll have to have lots more dates to enjoy the journey between those banks toward our destination. I'm in!" said Mark lovingly as he leaned over and put his arm reassuringly around her. They both lay back on the grass and stared up into the blue sky. The water rushed gently beside them, and two clouds scurried across the sky."

"They're following us, those clouds," murmured Jessica.

Suddenly there was a honking sound and the two Egyptian geese landed close to the couple, caressed each other and then plunged into the river in a flurry of feathers.

"It's up to us now," said Mark.

"I'm in!" said Jessica softly, as she smiled up at Mark and noticed that the two clouds had gone.


The End

# Romantic Farm

Ruth and her husband Peter relaxed for a moment during their exhausting day moving into their new home. They were very excited at having finally achieved their dream of buying their own home. Well, to be quite honest the bank had "bought" their home on paper and they would be paying for it for the next 20 years, but Ruth convinced herself that paying double her previous rent amount each month to the bank was still better in the long run than paying rent to a landlord, as they would eventually own this home. But 20 years did seem like a very long time right now!

She and Peter sipped quietly on their tea. As her kitchen-ware was still packed away in one of the big boxes that they were tackling one step at a time, she had had the foresight to purchase a cheap kettle and some tea so that they could at least stop every now and then for a cuppa and a break during the process of unpacking as they slowly got their new space set up that was going to soon be called home.

Although Ruth was really happy that she and Peter had finally found a home where they could settle, she still had a restless feeling. Ruth was essentially a farm girl. She had grown up on a farm outside of Impendle village in KwaZulu-Natal. The name of the village, Impendle, was a Zulu name meaning "uncovered" or "exposed", referring to a hill west of the town. Her childhood days had been spent in wide open spaces with gentle hills and mountains in the distance. One of her favourite walks was out to the natural waterfall that splashed heavily into a deep pool. Here was tranquillity and a sense of harmony with nature that she had simply not duplicated anywhere else in the world, despite having travelled to some extent with her husband Peter.

She had memories of riding horses up into the more mountainous area with her 2 brothers, and of cold winter nights where they would gather as a family around the anthracite stove in the kitchen where it was still warm. As a young girl she was soothed to sleep by the throbbing of the generator that provided the power needed to run their farm house, and which would cut out and go dead in the night when the rest of the household settled to sleep. Her father had passed away from a brief but virulent illness when she was still fairly young and her strong mother and 2 older brothers had continued to keep the farm running.

As the years passed, she and her brothers grew older and they went off to boarding school in their high school years as there was no school close to their remote farm. Her brothers went to study agriculture so that they could one day take over the farm, but misfortune struck and nature, which provided the tranquil beauty of the hilly walks and her favourite waterfall spot, also brought a cruel drought to the whole area which they never fully recovered from financially. In the end, her mother had to sell the farm and her brothers found work elsewhere. David became a manager of a wine farm in the Cape and Doug stayed on at the Agricultural College near Pietermarizburg as a lecturer. Her mom eventually re-married and settled with her new husband in Hilton, a small town on the outskirts of Pietermarizburg. Ruth had a good mind on her and won a bursary to study a business degree at Wits University in Johannesburg. Given the family circumstances, she didn't see that she had any other option but to avail herself of this opportunity to make it in the big wide world.

So these changes closed the chapter on what seemed now like an idyllic childhood where she had felt freer as a being than at any time since in her life. She assumed that this loss of freedom was what people called "growing up" and resigned herself to a different life in the hectic world of business and bills once she'd completed her business degree at Wits. One piece of good fortune about her move to Johannesburg was meeting Peter, who was her university sweetheart and soul mate.

So now she and her hubbie were about to settle into their little home in a middle-class suburb of Jo'burg. The house was in a "secure estate" which meant that there were another 19 houses of similar size but fortunately not all exactly look-alike, ensconced within a perimeter of fencing that had enough electrical voltage in it to severely shock any intruder who dared to enter the premises. This was Jo'burg's version of the modern day "moat". It was therefore "secure" and extremely un-tranquil and very far from harmonious with nature. But as Ruth and Peter had discussed, this was Jo'burg with its interesting set of modern problems and it seemed like the best way to go when hunting for the house of their dreams. Ruth preferred the noise of a vigilant German Shepherd on the farm to high-voltage electricity as her means of keeping intruders out but again, she resigned herself to the fact that things were different now and she was in a different world.

Thus, here she was, downing the last bit of tea as she and Peter sat on their heavy boxes containing their life's possessions in the empty shell of their new lounge. Tea break over, they got back to work. It was going to be a long day, so there was no point in delaying the tasks at hand.

Within a week or so, things were normalizing and the house was starting to feel like "home" for Ruth and Peter. They were able to take their attention off all the unpacking and got into the more creative phase of making it more beautiful with new curtains and landscaping their small garden. They got to know certain of their neighbours and started to settle in. Both Peter and Ruth were very career-minded and soon they were back to their busy schedules and getting on with business as usual. The hectic life was sweetened now with being able to come back home at the end of each day to the little nest they were creating in suburbia.

As the years passed by, Ruth bore Peter 2 children who attended the best schools due to their parents both being hard-working professionals who wanted the best for them. Their children, Pierre and Judy, grew up in a world totally different to the upbringing that Ruth had had, but as her childhood home had been sold long before she'd met Peter, she had never had the opportunity to show her children her childhood haunts. They were simply cherished memories that belonged to her, but which she did share with her children when there was time in the busy Jo'burg life to sit around a dining room table and chat about old times. Her mother passed away peacefully in her Hilton home and so there was not even reason to take her children down to that area to see their grandmother anymore.

Peter was a thorough-bred Jo'burger. He'd grown up close to the city and didn't have any clue what it was like to grow up with big, open spaces and the freedoms that Ruth had known. He was a happy-go-lucky personality and took life in his stride. Out-going and friendly, Peter was liked by many and easy to get along with. Ruth considered herself lucky to have found such an easy man as her life-partner – especially in this concrete jungle she'd had to adapt to as her new home.

Caught up in the whirlwind of raising a family, holding down a career and keeping her marriage created, Ruth didn't have too much time to dwell on the restlessness she'd come to accept as a normal part of her nature. She just got on with life and its immediate demands and was relatively content.

Then disaster struck. The world's stock markets crashed overnight and within a few months, Peter lost his well-paying job in a financial company and Ruth's position was also threatened. The children were close to finishing their schooling but it was going to be a tough call to keep them there on one salary. The 20-year mortgage for their house had 2 more years to be paid and that too was under threat. Due to the economic climate and Peter not having a monthly salary, the friendly bank that was quick to give them their 20-year noose all those years ago was not quite so friendly now and were just sending legal letters about paying on time when they'd already paid double the original loan amount in capital and interest payments over the years that they'd been paying off their house. Something had to be done fast to prevent her happy little setup from falling apart for a second time in her life.

As Peter was so well-connected and resourceful, he wasted no time in working out a solution for their finances. This turned out to be a "lucky" break for him as he was forced to confront relying on himself and his own skills, rather than the favours of a huge corporate structure to be kind enough to pay him a salary each month.

In a fairly short space of time, while they both made things work out on Ruth's salary, he had managed by word of mouth to build up a consulting practice helping clients to manage their finances and gear themselves towards financial freedom. Having learned from his own experience of paying off a formidable house mortgage for most of his adult life, and then almost losing his house, he had some good, hard, real-life reality that helped him to help others escape the shackles of debt as fast as they could. Although he did house calls, a lot of his work was conducted telephonically and over the internet which meant he had more time to spend with his family. Misfortune was turned into fortune for Ruth's family and they learned to rely on their own abilities. It was a good lesson for them both.

But as a result of this, Ruth started to feel that old restlessness. She became dissatisfied with her humdrum existence and for the first time since childhood, she started sensing the lost freedom of those times. She saw how much more free Peter had become in running his own show and it made her start to think and to question the paths she'd taken in her own life. These changes and pressures from the outside world had stirred up old memories and triggered the restlessness that she'd been able to keep at bay or ignore during the years of creating a marriage and family. Her children were almost finished with their schooling and her husband now had a job he really enjoyed and was not dependent on a "boss" anymore. She now started to feel really trapped in the corporate world.

The time passed by again and Pierre went off to study agriculture as he had spent some time with his uncle David on the farm he managed in the Cape and Pierre, too, chose a life out of the city as his future. Judy had it all planned out and was au-pairing in England for a year to satisfy her urge to travel a bit and see Europe. After that she'd be attending a hotel school as this was her dream - to work with people and possibly run her own hotel one day.

Once the children had left home, the restlessness became almost stifling for Ruth. Peter, observing his wife's discomfort suggested that they take a break and do a trip into the Drakensberg Mountains and get some space and tranquillity. As Peter's business was now rolling along, and as they had more time now with the children out of the house, Ruth didn't take much persuading. So off they went to spend a good 2 weeks up in the mountains.

It was Ruth's favourite time of the year to be in the mountains, the tail-end of winter. There had been a recent snowfall on the 'berg which had powdered the far peaks. The laid-back country hotel they had chosen provided a perfect view of most of the range of the "Dragon mountains". Called the "Dragon Mountains" or "Drakensberg" by the early Dutch settlers, and "uKhahlamba" (the Barrier of Spears) by the Zulu people, this 300 kilometre long mountain range resembling the spine of a great, long formidable dragon brought back memories of horse-rides on her childhood farm with her brothers. They would ride far out into the hills to find the best spot to view part of this breath-taking range of powerful, awe-inspiring mountains. Ruth knew that the industry and wealth of Jo'burg depended to some degree on the splashing water sourcing rivers way up in these mountains. They weren't just something grand and daunting to behold. They had their place in the sun and their fabulous storms!

After several days of their stay, doing all the mountain trails and breathing in the fresh, icy morning mountain air, eating sumptuous, hearty, farm-style meals in the old-fashioned kitchen, sitting around a log fire at night in the rustic, family-run hotel they'd chosen for most of their stay, they decided to take a long drive around the surrounding villages and towns during the next day for a change of scenery.

They headed off along country roads, admiring the spacious scenery and just drove with no particular destination in mind. Soon, Ruth realized that they were headed in the general direction of her childhood home. She started to recognize some of the terrain and the view of the mountains became all too familiar. She got a thrill of excitement as she sensed that freedom that she'd long since forgotten. Peter mentioned that he had a client out in this area and checked with Ruth if she minded too much if he popped in for a "house-call". As they'd had quite a nice long break already, Ruth didn't object. Business was business.

They drove on at a relaxed pace, taking in the scenery as they meandered along the rural roads. Suddenly she felt her world turn upside-down as she saw they were headed in the direction of her childhood farm. She spotted the exposed hill that was the origin of the name Impendle. Romantic memories flooded through her mind and she felt overwhelmed with emotion. She opened her mouth to tell Peter but the words wouldn't come out. He put his hand briefly on her leg as they drove and said "I know," and smiled.

As they approached closer, she saw that the old barbed-wire fence and rusty gate had been replaced by a tall mesh fence and an electric gate with an intercom. Peter spoke into the intercom, announcing his name and saying he was here from Jo'burg to see them about the business proposal that had been discussed. Ruth couldn't believe what was happening. How had this happened, that Peter had found clients that were the owners of her childhood farm house?

She sat silently, not knowing quite how to handle this situation she found herself in. Her universe was awash with different emotions. Excitement at seeing the old, familiar sights - although changed through the growth that time brings about - sadness at the memory of loss when her family had had to sell their beloved homestead - confusion at the current situation she was experiencing, where her husband who had never been here was driving her down the familiar old gravel road towards her old home.

Finally, they arrived at the home she had grown up in. As they arrived at the old house, 2 German Shepherds bolted out, barking ferociously until the owners, Bob and Milly, came out and soothed the dogs. The barking gave way to tail-wagging and sniffing and licking of the clearly welcome visitors. Bob and Milly too, gave them a warm welcome and showed them inside. It was the same old structure, but had been modernized over the years. The kitchen had been completely re-done and many other changes had been made that had made the space more user-friendly, but had retained the charm of an old farm-house. She saw also that several thatch rondavels had been erected on the huge extent of property around the original house.

Bob and Milly offered them a cup of tea and Ruth felt very strange sitting down in the same space that had been her old family lounge, but which had a new look now. This was the weirdest thing that had ever happened to her. But strangely, she also felt an utter sense of relief that the restless sensation that had plagued her all through her adult years had dissipated.

The elderly couple explained that they had converted their home into a small bed and breakfast for city couples and families seeking a break and a retreat into nature and the quietness and tranquillity of farm life. They had maintained a small section of the farm - mainly for subsistence living and to provide for the scrumptious, old-fashioned farm breakfasts that were served in the huge kitchen where Ruth used to sit with her family around the old anthracite stove. But Bob and Milly had decided that they were growing too old to live on such a huge property and had bought a little retirement cottage in a complex in Hilton, just outside Pietermaritzburg.

Ruth listened with half an ear, wishing that she could just get out and walk to her favourite spot with the waterfall and see how that looked after all these years. She suggested that they meet with Peter alone if they wished to discuss their financial plans and their retirement and asked if it would be possible for her to excuse herself and go for a walk outside.

Peter stopped her and said "Honey, we need you in on the discussion as Bob and Milly's financial plans are woven up in our possible financial plans." We can take a walk together later if you want to and you can show me all your old haunts.

Bob and Milly stared at each other - they had not known that this was Ruth's childhood home. Peter hadn't told them because frankly, he had also not known with absolute certainty if this was it. But he had had a pretty good gut feeling when the couple had explained how it was situated and how the most popular walk for the guests at their bed and breakfast was the walk out to the waterfall and pool where guests found a sense of tranquillity away from the pressures of corporate life.

"What do you mean?" asked Ruth nervously. "What financial plans?"

"Honey, Bob and Milly are selling their bed and breakfast business and the farm along with it. We have first option," said Peter - now suddenly just as nervous as Ruth as he had kept this a secret and discussed it only with his children, wanting to break this news to her when she was physically back in the space so that she would have time to really think it over and see what was there in present time as opposed to her possibly over-romantic memories that might have been exaggerated due to time and the loss she had suffered.

Ruth stared at Peter in a stunned silence. "You can't be serious?" she gasped. "What about our house in Jo'burg that's just been paid off after 20 years? What about your job, my job?"

Peter then explained to Ruth that he'd thought all these things through and hadn't discussed them with Ruth yet as he'd wanted to see the home with his own eyes and see if this would also be a right move for him, should they manage to pull it off. Judy, their daughter, was more than willing to manage and run the bed and breakfast, and possibly expand it into a more viable business. Pierre was thrilled at the prospect of being able to develop the farmland back to its full potential after all these years of lying fallow. He had studied all the latest technology in irrigation and dams and the farm never needed to fail again due to a drought. Peter had more than enough clients that he could handle over a distance once they'd sorted out the internet connections - and besides that, he could make trips out to clients where necessary to keep his hand in in the corporate world. After all, he was now his own boss!

"And my job?" asked Ruth. Peter went on to explain that financially, if they sold their Jo'burg house they could buy this house for cash and have investments that would make it not necessary for Ruth to work unless she really wanted to, in which case she could see what she wanted to do either on the farm or via the internet.

This was rather a lot for Ruth to absorb all in one go. She'd lost this house and kept only the memories. She had closed the chapter on this part of her life. She and

Peter had worked hard for 20 long years to pay off the mortgage on their Jo'burg townhouse behind the electric fence. She'd adapted to Jo'burg life and the expectations of peers - she'd got used to highlighting her greying hair, doing her make-up for the corporate image, wearing the tailored suits to look the part. Now she was looking at giving up all of this to go back to her roots and start again. This was painful but also, in a way, exhilarating. She just didn't know what to say at this point. The three other people present in the room sensed her anxiety and let her be quiet for some minutes. Even the German Shepherds scuttled off and lay quietly outside on the "stoep" (veranda). Peter touched her gently on the arm, telling her that she didn't need to make up her mind right now. It was something they could work out, talk about, and take their time over. Bob and Milly were not in a rush.

Ruth started to feel "uncovered" and "exposed" - "Impendle" - as her emotions were clearly visible to all present.

"Let's walk!" said Ruth.

"You lead the way, Tour Guide!" said Peter.

And so, they ambled quietly along the paths she remembered so well. They were now even more well-worn with guests having meandered along these same paths while Ruth and Peter had been carving their path through life in the big city. Ruth knew exactly where she was going. As she contemplated the decision she needed to make, she thought about her life and friends in Jo'burg. As she thought about this, the restlessness returned. She'd learned to live with this feeling for so long that it was an old sensation but now it really pierced her consciousness, having returned after its dissipation a little earlier that day. She knew then that she didn't have too much more to think about.

They all walked slowly down the last winding section of path that led to the place of tranquillity of her youth. This was the spot where she had always felt at peace as a child and where she dreamed her romantic dreams. The mild thundering sound of the waterfall greeted their ears just as they turned the last bend and came out of the foliage. There it was - her quiet place that was noisy - noise on the outside, but quiet inside her own space. This was not outside Jo'burg noise - this was nature's noise. She stood and watched the water pouring down and started planning the dam she and Pierre would build further down the stream to ensure no more threats of drought. She thought of the city people she could take up this path to share in her tranquillity. She realized that the tranquillity was back. The restlessness was gone. The doubts and anxiety were gone. She wouldn't need to highlight her hair anymore. In this place, she could wear whatever she was comfortable to wear, she could grow old and grey gracefully, she didn't need make up. She was home.

"Tour Guide! That's what I'll do here!" she said triumphantly. Peter reached out to her and she embraced the romantic man of her dreams in the romantic place of her dreams, and now her dreams were real.

"Let's go and sign the papers," said Bob quietly.

The End

# Love and Hope

(A short, sweet, old-fashioned country romance)

Rosemary and Garth had eyes for each other. The whole town knew it. The older folk could always sense these things but they kept quiet about what they knew. Rosemary's friends saw the extra blush in her cheeks and Garth's group noticed he had that extra swagger in his step whenever Rosemary came anywhere near him.

Now today, only Garth's best friend, Jason knew where he would be taking his Rosemary for dinner that night. Garth made him swear to secrecy because he didn't want the whole town in on this important evening he had planned with Rosemary. He needed to tell Jason because Jason was going to be the chauffeur and would drive them to the secret venue. This was a big moment for Garth and Rosemary and Garth had done everything possible to make sure he would impress his lady love and give her a wonderful night out.

Rosemary was super excited about the dinner that she'd been invited to. She could hardly contain herself as she went shopping with her friend Sarah that Saturday afternoon. Sarah was helping her to pick a beautiful dress to wear so that she could look elegant and beautiful for Garth.

Her mother had taught her never to overdo it, as that was distasteful and men would be turned off. She wanted to look gorgeous, with a touch of the right make-up to accentuate her good points, but not to have a dress that was too low-cut or skimpy.

Sarah and Rosemary both knew when they set eyes on the perfect dress for tonight's occasion. It was a cool, yellow garment which hung in glorious flares from a low waist band. The neckline was modest and the sleeves came to just above her elbows. Sarah tried on the dress and it fit perfectly. Not too tight, not too loose. She swirled around in the boutique watching the layers of yellow flares twirl. Both girls giggled in delight that they had found the perfect garment for Rosemary's romantic dinner with Garth.

Now the evening was drawing near and the time was getting closer for Garth and Rosemary to meet. Rosemary was quivering with happiness and excitement. This was her first actual date with Garth, although it had been obvious to the whole town for some time that this moment was long overdue for the two of them.

As the ruby red sun sank slowly behind the hills, bringing an end to the bright day, Rosemary caught a glimpse of Garth making his way up the street. She gasped with delight as she saw that he had really dressed the part of her romantic beau. He sauntered confidently down the sidewalk in a very nicely cut suit. In his pocket, was a yellow carnation – Rosemary could have sworn it was the perfect match for her dress. She wondered if there was a "spy" somewhere amongst her friends or his. Was this Garth and Rosemary's date? Or was the whole town in on this dinner?

Well, she didn't give it another thought and didn't care anyway. Because tonight was her night, and this was about Garth and Rosemary. She felt her heart skip a beat as she caught sight of his handsome face drawing nearer. She couldn't take her eyes off his as he approached her gate. Rosemary skipped down the path towards her gate, unable to contain herself. She knew this was not very dignified. The gentleman was supposed to come up the path, ring the doorbell and wait while the lady kept him waiting just a tad. It simply wasn't going to be this way with Rosemary.

Fighting furiously with the gate latch, she finally tore it open and dashed out to trot the few paces that separated her and Garth on this cool, perfect summer evening.

"Hiya Rosebud!" smiled Garth, hoisting her into his arms in an enthusiastic bear hug. Rosemary squealed with delight as he called her by the pet name he used when he felt particularly happy and affectionate. They hugged each other as if they would squeeze all the air out of their bodies before he gently lowered her to the sidewalk.

Her eyes were misty with emotion and she felt as if she could burst with happiness. This was a moment that any young girl in love yearned for, and here she was, living in this moment. Garth looked down with gentle eyes at her happiness and he in turn felt as if he could soar up into the sky with elation. He looked at this beauty in front of him and admired the yellow dress. He had not seen it on Rosemary before and realized that she had made an extra special effort to look beautiful for their date.

"I love the dress, Rosebud! It's so flowy and free – looks happy like you and me!"

"Yes Garth," said Rosemary, looking lovingly up at this dashingly handsome man, "I also noticed that... um... well..." Rosemary stopped abruptly as she saw the crumpled yellow carnation in tatters, falling out of Garth's pocket. She held her hand over her mouth and went into fits of laughter, unable to express how hilarious this looked – after all the trouble that Garth had gone to with his well-cut suit and taking the trouble to put the flower in his pocket.

"Ooh, I'm sorry, Garth, I just saw your carnation. It looked so stunning as you were walking down the road, but I'm afraid that in our embrace, it got a little mutilated!"

Garth looked at his pocket and the squashed flower and started to laugh merrily along with Rosemary. He pulled out the stem in a flourish and shook the loose bits over the side-walk, creating a yellow rain of petals falling onto the ground.

They laughed together and walked briskly down the road. Rosemary had no idea where they were going for their date. This was Garth's surprise for her and she let him lead the way.

Just around the corner, Jason was waiting in his big blue ford. He leapt out of the driver's seat and gallantly opened the back door for Rosemary to get in. Garth sat next to her on the other side and Jason climbed back into the driver's seat.

"We have our own personal chauffeur!" said Rosemary delightedly. "I hope you are not also our chaperone!"

"Oh no, Rosemary, I'll be dropping you two love-birds off at your destination and you can text me when you are ready for pick-up. I have other things to do than watch over you two. You just go and have a super evening, see?" said Jason kindly.

Rosemary and Garth held hands in the back seat as Jason's car rumbled along the country road. Suddenly, the car stuttered and jolted and despite desperate efforts by Jason to nurture the engine back to life, he had to eventually yield to its temperamental fit and slowly glided it to the edge of the road and stopped in a safe spot.

"Oh no!" exclaimed Garth with horror. This was his dream date with Rosemary gliding to a solemn halt at the side of the deserted country road. "Jason, can you fix it? This is my and Rosemary's big night, Jason! How could this be happening to us?"

"Garth, I really don't understand it. She was serviced just a couple of weeks ago and has been running fine. I promise you I wouldn't have offered to be your chauffer if I thought my car was unreliable. We'll see if we can get her going again," said Jason sorrowfully.

"Hey guys, it's fine! We'll make lemonade!" piped up Rosemary from the back seat.

The two young men looked at her with disbelief. "What do you mean, make lemonade? It's night time and we're stranded and there are no lemons or sun or lemonade stand out here that I'm aware of!"

said Garth in amusement at Rosemary's unexpected response to the turn of events.

"You see, Garth, my grandma always taught me that when life deals out sour lemons, you look for how to make some sweet and delicious lemonade out of those lemons. C'mon guys, look around you. The sun has set but there's still a glorious red streak along the horizon. Isn't that beautiful? And besides, if you look a bit higher, you'll see that there's a large and full moon shining up there already so you'll have some light to see your car engine. And apart from that, it's really an awesome sight up there in the wide-open sky. See! All those things that I've noticed in a few seconds are lemonade. Those are good things. So, the car broke. We have to make a plan. But don't lose sight of all the good stuff around. We can treat this as an adventure!"

Garth looked at this pretty girl next to him and felt a surge of happiness that he had selected her out of many pretty girls in town. He knew it already, but in this moment realized again that she was not just a lovely looking girl. She also had some extra special qualities that would help him along in his life, just as he would like to keep her happy and help her in her life. He started to feel better about the car and felt very right about his choice of a date partner. He also knew that Jason would never have purposefully sabotaged his evening. Rosemary was right. They needed to embrace the problem they faced and find the positive in things and it would all turn out OK.

Garth and Jason leapt out of the car to look at the engine and determine what could possibly be wrong. Rosemary too, peered in and looked at all the fascinating pipes and metal pieces which made up this engine. She held out her mobile phone to shine extra light on the intricate workings while Jason fiddled around and got a lot of grease all over his hands.

"I'm phoning Jake," said Garth a little impatiently. Jake worked at the town garage and knew a lot more about cars than Jason.

Jason agreed that was a good idea because he was not really going anywhere with his explorations into the engine. He tried the usual things that he knew but no matter what he pushed or pulled or adjusted, each time he tried to turn the key in the ignition, the car simply started with a jolt, then it petered out.

"Jake can come through in a while," said Garth, with relief, after speaking quickly on his phone. "He should be here within half an hour."

"Hey, I'm so sorry, you two!" said Jason. "I know this was your special night out. Now you have to hang around with me while we wait for Jake!"

"That's OK Jason. If you are one of Garth's best friends, I might as well get to know you better. After all, if Garth and I are going to be doing more stuff together, I'll have to like his friends. I know already that Garth likes Sarah, my best friend and they've known each other for a while. It's time I got to know Garth's friends too."

Once again, Garth was stunned at Rosemary's positive outlook on things. Here she was, caught in a predicament on their first date and she just kept seeing the bright side of circumstances. He was really warming to this gorgeous girl that he had decided to date.

"Let's play the lemonade game," he said suddenly. "You know, like Rosemary said – turn the lemons into lemonade or find the silver lining in the cloud. I need to get better at it if I'm going to date Rosebud here. She's a natural!"

"Well, guys, my grandma taught that to me when I was a very small girl. I've had years of experience! But I'm happy to help you guys catch up! I like that idea. OK so I'm first then. We have a whole 29 minutes now for me to get to know both of you better! If Garth and I were already at the restaurant on our date, I'd be enjoying getting to know Garth better. But we have possibly a whole lifetime ahead of us to get to know each other. The chances of me spending 29 additional quality minutes tonight with Jason are small. So we made a whole glass of lemonade there! I get to know your friend early on in our relationship. I already learned that he's kind and helpful and that he doesn't know too much about fixing cars. All very useful information," chuckled Rosemary, her mischievous eyes twinkling in the moonlight.

"OK, OK – my turn!" butted in Jason. "So firstly, the same way that you can get to know me, Rosemary, so I can get to know you better. Just because you're now dating Garth doesn't mean I can't get to know you well. And besides that, I really liked how you pointed out all the beautiful things around us – the moon and the red-lined sky. I like that kind of stuff. I also noticed that with the breeze, everything smells really fresh out here – better than spending time down at the smelly pub. Thinking of these good points helped me to forget for a moment how embarrassed I am that I let you guys down with my silly car. But… I just thought about that and turned it into lemonade. I realized I'm a really lucky fellow to have my own car! I know Garth is still saving up and will own a really nice car one day but all I need to do is get old Gertrude here fixed up and I've got my own wheels again. Lucky me!"

Garth was flabbergasted. He never thought of Jason as someone who enjoyed stuff like the moon and the sky and a fresh night breeze. He realized it was his turn.

"Well, you guys have really cheered me up with your lemonades! I have to say that a little while ago I thought I was the unluckiest guy in town tonight, when I heard that spluttering engine. But right now, I see that I just won the biggest jackpot life could ever offer me. I found out I chose a really, really nice, positive, happy girl to be my girlfriend. With Rosemary at my side, life can only get better and better. And I learned that one of my best friends has a romantic side to him – he likes the moon and stuff like that. That's so cool. The car breaking down on our important night has turned out to be one of the best things that has ever happened to me."

Before they knew it, the half hour had passed by and they were all laughing and sharing the happiness of their experience with each other. Jake couldn't believe what he saw when he pulled up with his truck. He thought they'd be annoyed and upset. But he found this happy trio looking as if they were having the time of their lives.

He proceeded to give the car a look-over with his strong torch light and soon figured out what the glitch was. After poking around in the engine and adjusting something, he turned the key and everyone cheered with delight as the engine of old Gertie roared with life. Jason was soon dropping off Garth and Rosemary for their dinner date at the country hotel outside of town.

And that was the start of Garth and Rosemary's first official date and a happier time for everyone. They became an inseparable couple and the older folk no longer had to keep quiet about what they knew. Sarah was happy for her friend and loved the fact that she had been in on the first secret about the yellow dress and had managed to sneak the message to Garth just in time so that he could get a yellow carnation to wear in his top pocket. Yellow was Rosemary's favourite colour – her happy colour. And Sarah liked to think she had something to do with this blossoming romance.

Before long, the whole town knew about the "lemonade" game and this little town was always looking on the bright side, no matter what hardships came to test their lemonade-making skills.

Rosemary's grandma would have been proud of her granddaughter. Rosemary had injected happiness and hope back into the little town and the lessons she had taught her granddaughter lived on beyond her lifetime.

Garth and Rosemary were soon married in the old, stone church. They were showered with yellow carnation petals as they came out of the church into a bright and sunny day, to start their married life together amongst their friends.


The End

# From the author:

Thank you for joining me in my world of romance and ideas. I hope that some of my stories have enhanced your life in some way.

If you enjoyed this book of short stories, I would appreciate it if you could review it on Amazon

Please check out my novel on my Amazon Author Page - *A Love Story from the Heart*

You will also find some more short stories that are not included in this book on my Amazon Author Page

Happy reading!

Contact Details:

Please contact me at:

terryatkinsonauthor@gmail.com

You can see my other books at:

www.terryatkinsonbooks.com

Made in the USA
San Bernardino, CA
25 March 2020